BRIEFLY SHORTS

Verity Donovan

ARTHUR H. STOCKWELL LTD
Torrs Park, Ilfracombe, Devon, EX34 8BA
Established 1898
www.ahstockwell.co.uk

First published in Great Britain, 2017

British Library Cataloguing-in-Publication Data.
A catalogue record for this book is available from the British Library.

ISBN 978-0-7223-4699-0
Printed in Great Britain by
Arthur H. Stockwell Ltd
Torrs Park Ilfracombe
Devon EX34 8BA

CONTENTS

A RELUCTANT BRIDE

Carrie and me – we played a game on our way to Longroyd's Mill. We dashed our metal-rimmed clogs against the stone setts to see who could get the biggest sparks. I usually won. Carrie was short and a bit on the heavy side, not built for the energy it took to chivvy the stones.

This morning she didn't look well. It was November and dark when we went to work, but under the gaslight her round face had a waxy glint.

"You all right, Carr?" I asked, feeling a bit anxious.

"Aye, as right as I'll ever be," she answered shortly.

She wrapped her woollen shawl closely round her plump shoulders. An early winter wind had suddenly surged up Dixey Street, straight off the moors. A lazy wind our mam always called it, on account it went straight through you instead of round.

We clocked on in silence. Soon the combing machines made any conversation impossible.

Just before the first break, at nine o'clock, I saw Carrie run round her machine and head for the toilets.

"She's been sick," mouthed Elsie Braddock. Elsie was a lot older than the rest of us, and kept a motherly eye on the girls.

Carrie came out, wiping her mouth on the corner of her black overall, just as the machines died.

We all sat on the floor, backs against the soft bales of wool, and ate our snap.

"I'm up the spout again," Carrie said suddenly. I'd noticed she hadn't eaten her bread.

I turned, feeling a sudden cold shock. "Never!"

"Aye, it's true," she intoned heavily.

"Whatever were you doing to get caught again!" I cried.

"Same as last time," she muttered.

"Oh, Carrie, not Billie again!" I wailed.

She looked indignant at that. "Well, it wouldn't be anybody else, would it!"

"How far gone are yer?" I asked, looking down at her stomach. There was one thing about being fat, you could hide the news you were carrying for some time.

"Three months," she replied gloomily.

I thought about her predicament. She already had an eighteen-month-old son by Billie Rowbotham. Billie was a right Jack the Lad. Fancied himself as the Prince of Wales with his quiff and white silk muffler he liked to call a scarf. Well, Carrie was no Wallis Simpson, but Billie seemed taken with her, and no mistake. The trouble was, Billie was work-shy. Never seemed to hold down a job – in fact, as far as I knew he'd never had a job, much to Carrie's disgust.

When we finished work it was already dark again. A sharp frost rimed the rooftops, and smoke from the night-shift factory chimneys belched upwards, ghostly white plumes against the darkening sky. After the heat of the mill, the cold air was a welcome change. We breathed in, savouring the sharp air, redolent with the pungent smell of wet wool rising from the grids, and, somewhere beyond, the aroma of fish and chips.

We shared two penn'orth of chips as we walked home, although we knew both mams would have a tasty stew waiting.

"Do you want me to come in with you when you tell your mam?" I said through a mouthful of hot chips.

"Nay, it's all right," she answered.

I felt a cowardly relief at that. I'd been with her when she told her mam the first time round. Mrs McGinty was of Irish stock, with a nasty temper. But I remembered that, when she'd eventually calmed down, propriety had taken over.

"Holy Mother of Jaysus, what will the neighbours tink?" she'd cried.

"Damn the neighbours," Carrie had said bluntly. "Billie Rowbotham hasn't worked since he left school. I'll wed him when he gets a job, not before. I'm not keeping him as well as a bairn."

I could see her point, and couldn't help admiring her for it. The trouble was that even with the arrival of little Billie junior his father hadn't bothered to get a job. It seemed that Carrie and Billie had reached stalemate.

But fate was about to take a hand, which is perhaps just as well in the scheme of things.

Because of the risk of fire from the greasy wool, we weren't allowed to smoke in the mill. So before the dinner break the next day, I was in the toilets sneaking a crafty ciggy.

Suddenly, I heard shouting, and then the machines stopped. Now, combing machines never stopped at this time of day without good reason, so I knew something was up. Out I ran, almost bumping into Elsie, who was hurrying past, ashen-faced.

"It's Carrie. One of the belts broke and hit her," she gasped.

I went to see her at the hospital after work. The bruise and swelling on Carrie's forehead had spread to most of her face by now. She'd been lucky. The leather belt which had broken away from the overhead wheels could have killed her.

"She'll be right as rain again, so the doctor says," Mrs McGinty assured me, rocking little Billie on her lap.

But big Billie was leaning over the bed looking anxious, fair hair slicked up as usual, and white scarf swinging forward.

He swallowed nervously and looked at Mrs McGinty. "I've got a job," he mumbled. "Start Monday at Sugden's Mill."

He looked at the still form of Carrie. I could feel the atmosphere round the bed grow tense. He then put a hand in his pocket and brought out a ring, slipping it silently on to the finger of Carrie's hand lying prone on the sheet.

"It belonged to me gran. It's yours now, love. We can get married just as soon as yer better."

I could see Carrie's mother holding her breath. Mr McGinty knew better than to open his mouth at all.

"Oh, aye." Carrie's voice was surprisingly strong. She suddenly opened her eyes and lifted her hand to look at the little ring with its garnet stone. "Well, I'll marry you on one condition, Billie Rowbotham," she said.

There was a hiss of exasperation from Carrie's mother.

"What condition is that, then?" Billie asked anxiously.

"On condition you get rid of that bloody muffler," she replied, closing both eyes again firmly.

HENRY'S OAK

Henry and the old oak went on the same night. She could hear the ferocity of the gale outside, an express train that thundered across the rooftops smashing everything in its wake. The windows rattled frenziedly and dislodged slates thumped and bounced overhead. The storm's noisy journey eventually ended with an explosion of sound, a finale that seemed to rock the foundations of the house.

Inside, the room was strangely quiet. She watched as the prematurely aged face turned to wax on the pillows, the mouth sagging open. She felt nothing. Even the anger had melted away months ago. She was like some empty crustacean with only space inside a hard shell.

She sat silently, hands calmly folded, gazing at the familiar yet unfamiliar face, until dawn drew a grey line around the window. Only then did she lift back the heavy curtains.

The oak lay in an undignified mass across the expanse of lawn. Black branches stretched across the grass and over the still sleeping flower beds. Its thick serrated trunk had been snapped like a twig. Her first thought was to wonder at the strength of the wind that had done that.

Henry had loved the tree – in the days when he had been able to feel emotion. She was suddenly glad he was no longer there to see the devastation. She continued to peer out, nose pressed to the icy glass. The tree looked helpless, abandoned, its inhabitants probably having fled before it fell. At least she hoped so.

She turned back into the room and moved to the bed. Henry didn't look any younger or at peace, as she'd heard people did when they died. He didn't look like Henry at all – at least not like the man she had been married to for all those years.

In recent months, she had often gone over the scenario of his eventual death, visualising in her mind how he would be in his final hours, how she would react. He would whisper her name, remembering it at last, and she would be kneeling before him, overwhelmed with grief.

But it hadn't been like that. He had gazed at her, a fierce, blazing expression in his watery blue eyes. He hadn't known who she was, even to the end. There had just been this silent rage between them.

They had staggered around blindly in a thick, unassailable fog for a long time before Henry's final illness. Two lost souls each unable to find the other, and in the end the one who had known everything had been unable to comfort the one who had been totally unaware.

Before they stopped coming to the house, friends had said what a shame it was about Henry, struck down in his prime.

"Look, Helen, if you need us at any time, don't hesitate, just pick up the phone. You know where we are," they had said, retreating quickly to the door.

She had nodded mutely, but inside her head she had been screaming. 'I need you now, please. Don't leave me alone with this strange, silent old man.' But they had disappeared, hardly daring to glance at Henry sitting gazing into space in his armchair.

It was almost as if they thought Alzheimer's was catching.

'You won't get it, you know, if you just call round now and again and talk to him. He just needs some company. I need company,' she had silently implored.

There were the usual sympathetic phone calls, of course, and some even brought flowers in the beginning, but they never really brought themselves. It was as if they had to don a special mantle, a protective coating against Henry. There had been a forced joviality, a false brightness that had been as hard and shiny as armour plating.

"Please leave your armour at the door as you come in," she wanted to shout. But instead, she had relented, offering coffee, sandwiches, anything to keep them there just a little longer, to make the visit a little less of an ordeal for them. It wasn't their fault, she reminded herself. They remembered Henry as a bright, fifty-something executive. They didn't understand. She didn't understand either, so how could she blame them for their insensitivity? No one liked to be reminded of old age. It was supposed to be a gradual process, not something that happened in two or three years.

"How are you, then, Henry, old fellow?" they would ask with that false jollity, eyes hardly daring to take in the bent figure rocking slightly in his chair.

They had spoken in loud voices, as if by doing so they could break through the confusion of Henry's mind. But it had merely frightened him, or made him angry.

Sometimes anger would override the confusion. "Bugger off, you silly sods!" he would rage.

She would smile then at their embarrassment, counting the seconds before they hurriedly made their excuses and fled.

Henry had been her best friend. They had often done the same things at the same time. They had laughed at this strange telepathy between them, but as Henry's illness progressed the communication between them had slowly died. For a time she had continued long conversations with him, but there had been no response from the vacant eyes. After a while she had grown as silent as he, wrapped up in an all-consuming grief.

Sometimes the grief was mixed with anger. She had wanted to kill him, this pathetic old man who had supplanted her dear, warm Henry.

But occasionally there had been a good day, when for a few

moments his eyes would suddenly clear like an early morning mist clears from a meadow on a summer's day. He would recognise her and smile Henry's smile that would melt her heart. For a few moments their fingers would entwine in mutual understanding. But only for a moment. When she looked again, Henry had gone and she would be alone once more with an old man she didn't recognise.

Mealtimes had become an ordeal. Sometimes it had taken more than an hour – an hour of trying to spoon food into a slack mouth, hearing the click and grind of teeth trying to manage the art of mastication.

On bad days he would hit out, refusing the food and throwing it against the wall, refusing to allow her to wash him or go near him.

It was then she thought she was going mad. She had become obsessed with bad smells – the smell of urine, of vomit, of old age itself. With the washing machine belting along in the early hours of the morning, she could still smell the odours she had just spent hours trying to eradicate. The shock and grief she had felt in the beginning had been compounded into this obsession with smells. But there had been many obsessions, among them the obsessions with daily living, and of dying.

Her one salvation then had been the oak tree. It must have been a couple of hundred years old, and for fifty of those a part of Henry's life.

He had grown up with the oak standing tall and strong in the middle of the lawn of his parents' house. He had swung on it as a child, carved his name on it in adolescence, and in his final years had taken comfort from its shade on hot summer days.

That last summer she had often wheeled him out to sit under its leafy canopy. It was the only time she had had any real peace. It was the only time that Henry had seemed at peace with himself. With Henry under the tree, she had been able to forget for a short time the grinding weariness and loneliness of caring for him.

Now Henry was gone, and she couldn't feel anything, not even relief. She knew she should feel that at least.

She closed the bedroom door quietly, as if afraid of disturbing him, and moved down the stairs, a dry-eyed ghost.

In the garden she caught her breath at the extent of the damage. The tree seemed to fill the lawn, and between its branches she could see many broken slates. What looked like someone's garage roof hung at a crazy angle from the top of a distant garden fence, which swung loosely in the light breeze. At least they had some garden fence. It appeared that many of their neighbours had lost theirs.

She moved to the broken, jagged trunk, and ran a loving hand along its rough bark. Henry would have been devastated to see the end of his beloved tree. It seemed fitting somehow that they had gone together.

They took away the oak on the day of Henry's funeral. As she slipped into her coat she could hear the long whine of the electric saw as it dissected the tree into neat logs.

She travelled in the funeral car with Henry's sister, Betty. She was only two years older than Henry, but the two had never been close. She lived in Leicestershire, and spent the entire journey complaining about the crowded train she had travelled on to get there. The seemingly endless chatter barely rippled the surface of the widow's consciousness.

Standing in the tiny chapel she wondered for one crazy moment what she was doing there. It was impossible to imagine that the little coffin they wheeled in towards the altar, topped with a spray of yellow rosebuds, actually housed Henry. For one thing, the coffin was too small. Henry had been a big man. How absurd to think he could shrink to the size of a small boy.

When they left the chapel it was raining. People huddled round the side entrance of the crematorium to look at the flowers and messages of sympathy. Calmly she picked up the spray of roses. The rest of the blooms would eventually be taken away by the crematorium staff, as she had been told the hospitals no longer accepted them.

Back at the house, a few friends and neighbours were grouped around drinking coffee and eating sandwiches, speaking in lowered tones. Only one or two accepted the glasses of sherry she proffered, although Betty managed three glasses before leaving by taxi to catch her train. The mourners then left one by one, giving her a comforting hug or a sympathetic pat on the back. Some of them had been Henry's work colleagues, and she noted the look of consternation and fear on some of the faces. It could happen to anyone, what had happened to Henry, and they knew it.

Then she was left alone again – alone with her thoughts and the soft patter of rain on the roof. Gently she picked up the yellow blooms and moved into the dripping garden.

The tree surgeon was busy packing away his equipment. All that remained of the oak was a scattering of twigs and little heaps of sawdust across the grass. But there was still the jagged trunk.

"I'll get rid of that tomorrow, if you like," the man offered.

She demurred. "No, leave it where it is. It belongs here. Henry would have wanted it that way."

The man shrugged. "Please yourself. I don't expect it will stop the young 'un establishing itself."

Her eyebrows rose. "The young one?"

"Yes, there." The man pointed to a young sapling no more than three feet high, standing proudly a couple of yards from its parent oak.

"Give it a bit of encouragement and you'll have another fine oak to take its place one day," the man ventured.

Wonderingly, she touched the tips of the young tree. Why hadn't she noticed it growing there? Then, turning, she gazed in sorrow at the broken trunk. Moving forward, she gently placed the roses at its base, where Henry's ashes would be scattered.

Only then, when the task was done, did she finally allow the tears to fall, and to blend with the rain on her face.

CANAL BY MOONLIGHT

Most nights, when it wasn't raining, she reached the canal bridge just on eight o'clock. It had to be the bridge. The rest of the road between Ogden's butcher's and Bank Street was a bit on the dark side. But at the canal bridge there were more gas lamps so people could see the wall. Over the years, a few drunks and the like had tipped over the low wall, never to be seen again.

"That canal should be drained. It's full o' disease wi' dead cats and such, not to mention t'fellows from the Tin Whistle peeing in it. Disgraceful, I call it." Aunt Edie's voice rose with righteous indignation. She didn't hold with strong drink didn't Aunt Edie. The work of the Devil she called it. But Betsie suspected her membership of the Band of Hope was more to do with Joseph Ramsden, one of the stalwarts there, than her love of teetotalism.

Aunt Edie was a widow, but she didn't intend staying so for long. She'd set her cap at Joe, and it was just a matter of time before he succumbed. Men were like that, she told her niece – soft dough in womenfolk's hands.

Betsie, walking carefully along the cobblestones towards the canal, wished that James Ogden was soft dough in her hands instead of an immovable piece of granite. The trouble was he was shy.

"A pound of sausages, half a pound of pig's cheek and a bit o' tripe, did you say, Miss?" was the nearest James, the butcher's son, got to holding a conversation with her. "That will be one shilling and twopence," he'd add stiffly, turning as red as the mound of stewing beef on the marble slab.

Betsie would hand over the money, heart pounding as his hand brushed hers. Shuffling her feet uncomfortably on the sawdust-strewn floor, she'd clear her throat and in a voice so high-pitched as to be scarcely recognisable reply, "Thank you very much."

This had been going on for months. The nearest thing she got to a conversation was to inquire after his father, who was ill with bronchitis.

James was having to run the shop on his own. Perhaps that was why he had been looking so preoccupied lately, Betsie thought.

Walking across the canal bridge, she got to know when James closed the shop. He usually made the bridge just after the nearby town-hall clock chimed eight. But tonight there was no sign of him. He must have closed up early.

Disconsolately, she retraced her steps across the bridge and walked back through Railway Street to Aunt Edie's back-to-back terrace house. It had been home to Betsie for the past five years since the death of her parents.

"You're back early, our Betsie." It was Tommy, Aunt Edie's son, who was sprawled in a chair in front of the range.

There was a strong smell of scorching cotton, and through the haze Betsie could see Aunt Edie, grim-faced at the kitchen table, banging away with a flat iron.

"Ee, what's up, Aunt Edie?" Betsie looked from smirking Tommy to the set face of her aunt.

Behind his mother's back. Tommy was silently mouthing, "Look on the table!"

Betsie, feeling somewhat apprehensive, gazed at the table, with its pile of freshly ironed clothes. Next to it stood what appeared to be a tall glass of dark brown liquid with a nice foamy head on it. As if to press home the message. Tommy rose, stretched out his hand and grasped the glass, holding it up to the light triumphantly.

"Milk stout!" he proclaimed gleefully. "Doesn't look like our mam will be going back to the Band of Hope no more." He swung the glass playfully from side to side in front of his mother's nose.

Aunt Edie whipped round and snatched the glass from him, slopping some of the contents on to the floor.

"I'll thank you to mind yer own business, Thomas Wood," she cried warningly, and, turning, swept from the room, slamming the kitchen door behind her.

"What's happened, then?" Betsie asked.

"Oh, me mam feels she's been slighted, or summat. That chap she's keen on – Joe what's-'is-name – seems to have taken up with Maggie Tripper." Tommy grinned and slumped back into the chair.

"Oh, no," Betsie said, dismayed. She knew how much store Aunt Edie had put into getting wed to Mr Ramsden and moving into his smart semi in Claybottom Lane.

"Do you mean Maggie Tripper who works behind the bar in the Tin Whistle? Joe's in the Band of Hope, so what's she doing bothering with him?" Betsie asked, looking puzzled.

"Nay, God knows!" Tommy shrugged. He bent and picked up the poker in the hearth and dug energetically at the coals, sending hot sparks coursing up the soot-encrusted chimney. "Says she's given up bar work. Says she's seen the light or summat. One thing's for sure, she's upset me mam and no mistake." He chuckled as he settled back in the chair again.

"I don't know what you're so pleased about, our Tommy," Betsie said crossly, tossing her brown curls. "It's no joking matter. If Auntie doesn't get wed, she'll expect me to stay here."

"Ee, that'll be a right shame," Tommy mocked. He knew Betsie had set her heart on moving into a room in the home of her best friend, Florrie, on the other side of town. Florrie's mam had a bathroom and inside toilet – unlike Aunt Edie, whose privy was several yards up the street.

It wasn't so bad in summer, but in winter it was an ordeal. With the wind howling and stirring up flurries of snow, Betsie often felt like Scott of the Antarctic as she struggled to the privy, armed with torn sheets of newspaper and a lamp. Remembering the icy wind blowing round her bare buttocks, she felt tears sting her eyes. first James Ogden hadn't turned up and now this.

"It's all right for you. You'll be getting wed to Mavis Thornton and going to live in that nice flat above the betting shop," she cried furiously, turning the disappointment she felt into anger against the hapless Tommy.

"Aye, well, we haven't made any plans yet – there's no hurry," he said, yawning.

"There never is with you," she retorted, beginning to unfasten her coat.

It was high time Tommy settled down, she thought. Mavis was a nice girl who worked in a hairdresser's in the middle of the High Street. Tommy, on the other hand, never seemed to settle to anything. At the moment he worked as a cleaner at the local woollen mill, oiling the machines and sweeping up bits of jute and wool from the machine-room floors.

"Sometimes I think you've got carpet fluff between the ears. Tommy Wood," she said with a resigned sigh.

"Who, me?" Tommy looked up in mock surprise. He never stayed serious for long, and at times he could be downright aggravating.

"Yes, you. It's high time you hurried up and married Mavis before she finds someone else with better prospects," she lectured.

Tommy looked thoughtful for a moment. "Aye, perhaps you're right, cousin. In fact, I've been thinking lately of joining the army like me dad did. I'm told they teach you a trade there."

Betsie didn't say anything, but sent up a silent prayer that things might come right for him. He'd had so many jobs and never stayed long at any of them. At least if he left and got married and joined the army, she would be able to have a room to herself instead of sharing with Aunt Edie, who often kept her awake at nights with her loud snoring.

She sighed, feeling suddenly despondent.

Tommy was looking at her keenly. "What's up, young Betsie? That Jimmy Ogden still playing hard to get? I bet you still haven't got past the 'good evening' stage when you pass on that canal bridge."

Betsie flushed, and eyed her cousin sharply. How did he know she went out to the bridge on the off chance of meeting up with Jimmy?

"None of your business," she mumbled self-consciously.

"You and Mam both. I can see it's going to be a laugh a minute round here with you two," he said in disgust. Then, suddenly brightening, he got up from the chair. "Come on, our Betsie, you need cheering up. Get yer coat on again, and we'll go out on the town. How about supper at the Bow Window? We can pick up Mavis on the way."

"What about Aunt Edie?" she ventured.

"We'll bring Mam something back," he countered. "Come on, lass, let's get going."

She suddenly felt much better. The Bow Window was a little eatery run by a local butcher, Mr Purvis, well known in the town for his sausages. It was a popular meeting place with its scrubbed wooden tables and sawdust floor. In striped apron and pork-pie hat, Mr Purvis presided over a black pot-bellied stove resting on a grid over an open fire. He provided the best sausages they were ever likely to taste, served in little white bowls with mushy peas. For an extra penny you could get a fresh muffin to dunk in the peas.

The thought of the feast to come made their mouths water as they hurriedly opened the door and stepped out on to the pavement. They almost fell over the burly figure of a man who had just been about to knock on the door.

"Er, hello, Tommy lad. Just going out?" The voice was deep yet nervous.

"Is that you, Mr Ramsden?" Tommy queried, feigning surprise.

"Aye, it is. I've come to see yer mother. Is she about?"

Tommy peered up at the middle-aged man. In the poor light from the street lamp he looked pale and strained.

"Well, she's in, but I'm not sure she'll want to see you," Tommy answered slowly.

"Oh, dear." Joe Ramsden sighed heavily and, removing his flat cap, mopped his forehead. "Ah think I 'ave upset her a bit. Maggie Tripper doesn't mean anything, y'know. I reckon I've been proper daft. I mean, it's yer mother I care about. I was only trying to help Maggie, her being a new member and me being t'secretary an' all." Joe was a big man, but he was shuffling about like an overgrown schoolboy.

Just then they heard the window sash sliding above, and Aunt Edie poked her head out from the bedroom. "What's going on down there? Is that you, young Tommy?

"Aye, Mam. I'm talking to Joe. He's come to see you, but I've told him you don't want to see him any more on account that you're jealous of Maggie Tripper." Tommy could hardly keep the laughter from his voice.

Betsie jabbed him in the ribs warningly.

There was a derisive snort from above. "You keep your nose out of things, our Tommy. I'm nothing of the sort. I'll be right down."

Within seconds Aunt Edie was on the step.

"What's this all about? What are you doing here, Joseph Ramsden?" Her tone was hardly encouraging.

"Ee, Edie, love. I just had to come round and sort things out, like. If I upset you, I'm sorry. . . ." Joe's voice trailed off miserably.

Aunt Edie looked pleased and embarrassed at the same time.

"You'd best come in, then," she murmured. Then, seeing Betsie and Tommy on the pavement, she glared. "Where are you two off to, then?"

"Tommy and me are taking Mavis to the Bow Window," Betsie stammered.

"Well, don't be long. You've both to get up for work in t'morning."

With that, she grabbed Joe's arm and bustled him over the threshold, slamming the door on the young pair.

"Well, that was soon sorted out!" Betsie exclaimed. "You certainly like stirring the pot. Fancy telling yer mam she was jealous."

Tommy laughed. "Well, it worked, didn't it? You see, they'll be announcing the banns before long."

"A right little matchmaker, aren't you?" Betsie mocked.

"When it's needed," Tommy replied loftily.

They walked on in companionable silence. The sulphurous smell of hot coke and brick dust prickled their nostrils. The nearby brickworks had opened a kiln that day, and a soft red glow suffused the night sky.

"Now all we have to do is get you sorted out," he remarked.

"Don't you dare, Tommy Wood," she warned. "I don't want you telling Jimmy Ogden that I'm jealous!"

"Well, you're not going to get anywhere with him when the only conversation you have is about the price of tripe!" he said bluntly.

There were times when, for all his jokey ways, Tommy could hit the nail on the head where it mattered most.

Then a thought struck him, and he began to laugh. "Ee, I hope me mam managed to get rid of that milk stout!"

The following night, Betsie didn't feel like walking to the canal bridge. Remembering Tommy's words, she felt disheartened. 'Maybe I'm wasting my time,' she thought gloomily. 'I'll never get past talking about tripe or the weather with Jimmy Ogden.'

But two nights later, with the full moon beckoning, she was tempted into buttoning up her coat and stepping out into the damp air.

"Just going to see Florrie," she called, as she always did.

Aunt Edie merely nodded. She had been in a good mood since Joe Ramsden's visit. There was something in the wind, and it could only be good news, Betsie thought optimistically.

As Betsie approached the canal once more, her footsteps slowed and her heartbeat quickened. It was a perfect night for a romantic encounter. She sighed. If only he would close his shop on time tonight!

The reflection of the moon shivered on the oily surface of the water. Its murky depths had been given a mysterious translucency, seen from the bridge. But she noticed clumps of reeds struggling to survive along the canal edge; and, on the bank, tufts of grass and straggly weeds grew between broken flagstones.

She heard the town-hall clock chime eight, and somewhere in one of the nearby streets with its huddled rows of back-to-back houses she heard a dog bark.

It was then she saw him on the far side of the bridge, the street lights turning his sandy hair a strange caramel colour in the greenish glow.

She quickened her pace across the bridge, her heart thumping and her mouth dry. The words were already forming on her lips as she approached the hurrying figure, when to her left she heard a splash.

Jimmy must have heard it as well, as, almost abreast now, they both simultaneously peered over the parapet. They could see the shape of a man running along the towpath, but it was the sack which he had obviously thrown into the water that drew their attention.

She heard Jimmy mutter, "Oh, no, not again!" He turned to look at her properly for the first time. "Some folks are heartless. This is the second time I've seen this happen in the last couple o' months," he said angrily. Then, grabbing her elbow he quickly urged her towards the low wall leading to the towpath. "Come on, lass, I need your help."

Willingly, Betsie allowed herself to be led over the wall and on to the path. All shyness between them appeared to have evaporated.

It was colder and damper on the canal bank, and surprisingly dark even with the moonlight. The dank air was redolent with the smell of rotting vegetation, and on closer inspection the canal side had swapped its romantic air for one of neglect and abandonment. But they could just see the sack bobbing up and down on the oily water.

"Here, you're lighter than me. If I hold on to yer legs perhaps y'can stretch over and reach. It's not too far out," Jimmy urged, already helping her down over the bank.

As he held on grimly to her waist, she stretched her arms over the water, fervently wishing she had been wearing her best silk stockings instead of the black woollen ones Aunt Edie insisted she wore.

'I'll be mortified if he sees me combinations,' she thought, through gritted teeth. But all thoughts of vanity and modesty vanished as her hands caught hold of the top of the sack.

"Got it!" she cried triumphantly.

But even as she spoke the weight of the sack began to drag her down, and Betsie found herself sinking with it. Jimmy hurriedly hauled her to safety. She never knew how much of the foul-tasting water she gulped down as she was lifted on to the towpath, still clutching the dripping sack.

From the waist up, Betsie looked like a half-drowned whippet, mud and weed sticking to her hair and coat. But for a moment her appearance was forgotten as Jimmy feverishly untied the rope from the neck of the rough sacking.

Turning the bag upside down, he emptied what looked like pieces of carpet cut-offs. Astonished, they both peered down at the pile of sodden rubbish.

"Is that what I nearly drowned for, James Ogden?" Betsie demanded, but she didn't sound too upset.

Jimmy shook his head. "Well I never! Still, I'm glad it wasn't a dog this time."

"This time?" Betsie echoed, her teeth beginning to chatter as she realised how cold and wet she felt.

"Yes, it's happened afore," Jimmy explained, removing his coat and gently placing it round her shoulders. "I rescued a sack from this spot a couple o' months ago. Got it in to the bank all wet and soggy, like; and when I opened it up, there was a greyhound inside. Almost on her last legs an' all."

"What happened to it?"

Jimmy smiled. "I've kept her. I call her Ropey on account she was all tied up."

The pair scrambled back over the wall again and on to the bridge, suddenly feeling at ease in each other's company.

"Best get you back 'ome before yer catch yer death," he said amiably, putting an arm around Betsie's shoulders.

"I don't know what Aunt Edie will say when she sees me in this state," Betsie said, but she didn't sound too worried.

Jimmy cleared his throat, appearing nervous again. "Look, I'll see you 'ome and explain to yer auntie."

"All right, then," Betsie agreed.

They walked on in silence, and then Jimmy nervously cleared his throat. "I was wondering. If you like dogs you might like to go a walk with me and Ropey sometime. How about tomorrow night?"

Betsie felt as if she was in some kind of dream and would wake up at any minute.

"That will be grand," she said happily, hoping she didn't sound too eager.

Silently she thanked Cousin Tommy, for she was sure it had been him she had seen running away along the towpath. Up to his matchmaking tricks again, no doubt!

Perhaps one day she would tell Jimmy and they would laugh about it, but not right now.

Jimmy, his arm comfortably encircling Betsie's waist, gave her a sidelong glance, and then looked away again quickly.

He must remember to pay Tommy Wood that half-crown he'd promised him. Maybe one day he'd tell Betsie what he'd done to get things moving – but not right now.

THE MAGIC KNIFE

Marcie Robinson was swinging to and fro on her garden gate. It was the only one in the street that worked properly. She was busy chewing, cheeks bulging and mouth gyrating.

"What you got there, then?" Eddie from next door asked. He was nine and small for his age.

Marcie gazed at him disdainfully as he sidled along the wall, scraping his grey pullover.

"A banana," she answered through her full mouth.

"A banana – what's that?" Eddie asked, eyes large and luminous in his pale face.

"It's fruit, silly," she retorted crossly.

"Can I have a bite?" But he already knew the answer. Largesse was not one of Marcie's finer qualities, yet the candle of optimism always burned brightly in Eddie's soul.

"Nah, but you can have the skin if you like."

Surprised at this sudden generosity, he took the strips of banana skin from her proffered hand. They smelled strange and yet somehow familiar, both at the same time. He scraped a dirty fingernail along the pale, fuzzy lining, and popped the resulting blob into his mouth.

It was slightly bitter, yet the smell had held so much promise of deliciousness. He suspected the actual fruit would taste much nicer.

Marcie Robinson had a banana, then?" his mother said later. She was busy fluffing out her wiry black hair in front of the mirror.

"Well, I can't afford any – not that I've seen any about. But you can get anything on the black market when there's a war on – if you've the money, that is."

She carefully drew a thin black line where her eyebrows used to be.

"Your father's only in the army, fighting for King and country. We're here, living from hand to mouth, but when you're a miner you can get anything." Her tone was bitter.

Eddie watched as she got ready to go to the Dog and Duck. She worked as a barmaid and he was used to spending his evenings, and sometimes all night, alone. He didn't mind being on his own. He could stay up late and listen to *Armchair Detectives* on the wireless. If he was frightened, then Uncle Chuck's knife would protect him.

He'd liked Uncle Chuck. He had laughed a lot and brought him chocolate and chewing gum.

Chuck was what his mother called a GI, and she had cried when they had posted him overseas. They wouldn't see him again. Before he left he had given Eddie the knife. It was only small, slightly smaller than a penknife, with a picture of a cowboy on the handle. Chuck had told him to keep it with him always. It had magic properties.

The gardens and rooftops were white with frost when Eddie got up for school the next morning. He dressed quickly and ran downstairs quietly so as not to wake his mother. She didn't get home until the early hours and wouldn't take kindly to him waking her up.

Eddie hated the cold mornings of late winter. He hated school. But most of all he hated Robert Green and Harry Robinson, Marcie's brother, who teased him in the playground: "Eddie

Bragg, Eddie Bragg, yer mother's a slag." His face burned at the memory of their taunts.

He helped himself to a slice of bread and dripping and then silently let himself out of the house. A biting wind cut through his thin clothing. He noticed the Robinsons had received another delivery of coal – a black mountain that spilled across the pavement.

"Fancy – a ton of free coal!" his mother had said in amazement. "Why couldn't your dad have been a miner?"

Eddie silently wished his dad had been a miner; then his mother wouldn't have had to work in the pub and he could have had as many bananas as he liked.

Once at school, Eddie was glad of the cold. His classmates were too busy trying to keep warm to worry him. The day moved along smoothly enough, and he got a gold star for doing his sums right.

But when the bell sounded for home time, Eddie realised he wasn't going to have an easy day after all. His heart sank as he saw Harry Robinson and Robert Green waiting for him at the school gates. They spotted him immediately, and began moving towards him chanting. Soon a small group of children had gathered to watch. Harry Robinson strutted up, thrusting his face close to that of the smaller boy.

"Your mother's dirt, Eddie Bragg. She goes with Yanks!" he hissed.

Then, without warning, he lashed out, sending Eddie crashing heavily to the ground. As he hit the gravel, Eddie felt a sharp pain in his side. He tried to get up, but the pain was too much. He put his hand to his side. There was a sharp gasp from the children gathered round, and someone in the crowd screamed.

"He's bleeding – Eddie's bleeding. Fetch the teacher."

In a daze, Eddie looked down. His hand was covered in blood. A dark red stain was spreading through his thin coat at an alarming rate, and before help could arrive he had fainted.

Eddie woke up surrounded by white, and wondered if he was in heaven. A lady in a tall white hat gazed down at him, smiling.

"You're a very lucky boy," she said gently.

Eddie felt frightened. "Where am I?" he asked tremulously.

"In hospital. You've got to lie still for a while as you have had some stitches. Your mother's here. She's been very worried about you."

His mother suddenly appeared at the foot of the bed, looking pale and anxious.

"You'll be all right, Eddie, but you gave us all a nasty shock," she scolded, but she looked relieved all the same. "Whatever made you carry that knife in your pocket? You could have been killed."

She came round and suddenly placed a large brown paper bag on the bed.

"Those boys who were bullying you got a right ticking-off. But all your classmates have sent a 'get well' card." She produced the card from the bag. "All the children signed it. Oh, and Mrs Robinson sent you these." She opened the neck of the bag further so that he could see the contents.

Eddie struggled up on one elbow. The bag contained several bright-yellow bananas.

He sank back, a gratifying smile on his face.

Chuck's knife really had been magic!

TRANSFORMING BETTY

Buxom Betty was well known amongst the haulage drivers who used the motorway services. Dressed in faded denims and a man-sized jacket, she was affectionately known as Big Betty, weighing in at almost twenty stone on a six-foot frame.

But she liked to be one of the boys, laughing and joking with the best of them as she downed giant portions of eggs, bacon, fried bread, baked beans, sausages and black pudding. She loved being part of her father's firm, driving twenty-tonners between Manchester and Dover, although she had set her sights on the forty-four-tonners in her father's fleet. After producing five strapping sons, Mrs Barker was delighted when her sixth child was a girl. But her attempts to dress Bettina in frilly feminine clothes became a real struggle when Betty got into her teens and showed every sign of taking after her brothers in size.

"Why couldn't she settle for being a hairdresser!" complained Betty's mother to her husband. "You're to blame for encouraging her to drive those big things. She's still a girl."

"She wants to be like her brothers, and she's shown she can handle the trucks, so that's the end of it," Mr Barker said firmly.

His wife knew when she was beaten.

In spite of her size, Betty was a pleasant-looking girl with a thick crop of blonde hair, and wasn't short of admirers. One in particular was John Coombes, one of the few drivers who could more than match Betty in size. A gentle, shy man, he kept his feelings for Betty under wraps – or so he thought. He knew he would be teased mightily by the lads he met up with from time to time in the motorway cafés. But his feelings for Betty had not gone unnoticed by some of the drivers, who would give the odd nudge and wink when Betty put in an appearance.

It was usually by chance that the drivers met up, and so it was a bright day in April when the usual group met up at a service station on the M1. Tony Dell, who worked for a firm in Blackburn, was accompanied this time by an athletic-looking fellow in his early thirties, sporting close-cropped sandy hair.

"Oh, aye, Tony, what have we got here, then?" Garry McCann called out, eyeing the newcomer cheekily.

Garry was small and slight, quite a bit older than the other drivers, but well respected for his skill on the roads in even the worst of weather.

"This is Terry Walters. He's taking over from me next week. I'm out. I've had enough of driving, and now they want me to do the Scottish run with two nights away. Marje doesn't like me being away one night, never mind two, so I've had it."

"We're sorry to hear that, Tony. We'll miss you, won't we, boys?" Garry said, turning to the other drivers who were busy eating their breakfasts. They all murmured assent, but if truth were told they would not miss Tony Dell too much. He was a professional moaner, and the hauliers wondered at a wife like Marje who would want him home more often.

"What are you going to do, then, Tony?" Garry asked.

"The wife's father owns a fish-and-chip shop and wants me to join him. I'm thinking about it," Tony replied.

"We'll be all right for a fish supper, then, if ever we are in Blackburn, eh, boys!" Garry grinned, winking.

"Well, that's if I take the job. Can't say I like fish and chips all that much, and the smell can stick to yer clothes. Marje's father always stinks of 'em." Tony didn't sound too thrilled at the prospect, but then he was never enthusiastic about anything.

The new boy went to the counter to get his meal, just as Betty arrived. Terry sat down with a loaded plate.

Betty looked at him questioningly, and then turned to the other drivers. "Aren't you going to introduce me, then?" she asked.

"Sorry, Betty," mumbled Tony. "I've just been telling the boys that Terry Walters here is taking over my run next week. Terry, this is Big, er, Betty."

Terry smiled at her as she held out her hand for him to shake, but Terry bent and kissed the proffered hand instead.

"Hey, you'll have to watch it, young Betty," laughed another driver, Sam Carter, a skinny little fellow who always looked lost behind the wheel of his truck, but who was surprisingly strong.

"I can take care of myself," Betty murmured, but the shy way in which she said it made the other drivers snigger.

"You'll have to watch our new boy, John," Garry said, turning to the big driver who had remained silent throughout. "That there Greek god is going to whip Betty from under yer nose," he added with a smirk.

Betty gave an exasperated snort, and all the drivers laughed. John, looking embarrassed, merely grinned and shook his head slowly. They all knew he was keen on Betty, but so far he hadn't made a move on her and it didn't look likely that he would any day soon.

It was another six weeks before the same drivers met up again in an M1 service-station café. Garry was the first to arrive, and whooped gleefully when he was soon joined by John, and the newcomer, Terry, followed shortly by Sam, the skinny one.

"This recession is a cow," grumbled Sam gloomily. "I've been laid off for the last three weeks. It was either that or get on me bike. First time out today, and I've had a cut in pay. Jenny's not bloody happy, I can tell you. We have two kids and she's had to go out to work."

"What does she do?" asked John, as the group made their way to the counter for their breakfasts and mugs of tea.

"Works part-time in the supermarket, and we can just about manage. I'm only glad to be on the road again this week." He turned to new boy Terry, who was just paying at the end of the counter. "What about you, Tel?"

For some reason, Terry looked slightly uncomfortable. "I'm not married, so no problem there, but I moved back in with my mother just before I got this job. I'm looking for a place of my own now, up Manchester way."

As they moved back to their usual table, one of the men looked round. "Wonder what's happened to our Betty, then? Maybe she's been laid off, along with Austin and Jack."

The drivers glanced at John, who shrugged and turned crimson. The drivers hooted with laughter as Garry slapped him on the back.

"Still got the hots for our Betty, eh, John?" he grinned. "Well, sorry, mate, but she's Terry's bird – if he wants her, that is." He looked expectantly across at Terry. Terry said nothing, but concentrated on his plate, looking relieved when Garry's attention was riveted to the door.

"Well, well, speak of the Devil," he retorted. All eyes widened as Garry gave a low whistle. "Cor, Betty girl, I wouldn't have known it was you, all tarted up, like!" he exclaimed.

There was no doubt Betty had changed. She looked a couple of stone lighter, the old faded dungarees replaced by a pair of navy jeans, topped by a floral blouse.

"You're a sight for sore eyes, gel. And what's with the lipstick? You'll have trouble with old John there if you're not careful."

The drivers laughed, and even John, who was looking shell-shocked, managed an embarrassed grin.

Betty smiled, taking in the compliments, as she made for the counter.

"Well, well, what about that, boys?" Garry said, looking round the table. He gave Terry a sly look. "I wouldn't be surprised if all that effort wasn't done for you, Tel boy."

Terry calmly pushed away his plate. "Lay off, Garry – you'll only embarrass the girl."

Just then Betty arrived with her breakfast, sitting down carefully at the end of the table.

"Holy cow, Betty, that wouldn't be enough to go in a gnat's eye," Sam yelled, looking in horror at the poached egg gracing the slice of dry toast that Betty had placed in front of her.

"Are you on a diet?" asked Terry, smiling at her in obvious admiration.

Betty looked slightly sheepish, but smiled back. "Not really; I'm just eating sensibly. This is much more healthy than all that greasy food," she said, looking meaningfully at the fried breakfasts the drivers were consuming.

There was silence for a moment, with John gazing down at his plate as if he had suddenly found something of great importance on its surface.

Terry broke the silence after taking a swig of his tea and setting the mug down with elaborate care. "Betty, I wonder if you would care to come to my birthday bash a week on Saturday?" He sounded as if he had come to some major decision.

Pandemonium broke out, as the drivers hooted with glee and banged the table.

"What did I tell you guys!" Garry laughed.

Betty seemed oblivious to the taunts. "I'd like to, Terry. Where are you having it?"

"It's at the Pink Dahlia, a club in Manchester, and you're all welcome to come, if you can make it," Terry replied, looking round at the other drivers.

Betty looked slightly disappointed, but said nothing. The others, however, were enthusiastic.

"I met up with old Trevor and Austin last week, and I'm sure they'd like to come," enthused Garry.

"I'm living in Burnley, so it's not far, and I'd like to see Trev again, so you can count me in," John said.

"Trevor's not on the road now," Garry explained. "He's gone to work for his cousin in a pub. Austin's still on the road, but he's covering the north-east at the moment."

"I'm sure it'll be a great night," Sam Carter beamed. "Thanks for the invite, mate."

The men began drifting towards the door.

"It's on June the 5th from eight o'clock on. It won't be formal, but don't turn up in those overalls!" Terry called.

Betty remained seated and toyed with the now congealing egg on her plate. John had remained behind, and was eyeing her uncomfortably.

"You're going, then?" he asked quietly.

"Of course I'm going!" Betty retorted, slightly irritated by his manner.

"I honestly don't think this club is the right place for you. . . ." John tailed off, looking embarrassed.

"Don't be so stuffy, John. It's a nightclub – so what! We'll have a great time, but if you're going to be such a misery guts perhaps it might be better if you don't come," she snapped.

She rose from the table, and marched towards the door.

"OK, have it your way. I'll pick you up in my car, seven thirty," John called.

Betty nodded curtly, and disappeared.

Betty's mother beamed with pride as she watched her daughter getting ready for Terry's party. She marvelled at the change in her daughter. Who would have thought she would ever see Betty dressed in black velvet tapered trousers and a pink blouse with frills? Make-up, too! She watched in awe as Betty applied two coats of mascara to the lashes of her bright blue eyes.

"You do look nice, Betty dear!" she exclaimed, patting her daughter's arm.

"Are you sure I look all right in this?" Betty asked anxiously.

"Betty, you look wonderful, and I know that young man

will think the same," she said.

Despite her assurances, she secretly felt apprehensive about this Terry that Betty had mentioned. It all seemed a bit too quick, but Betty appeared smitten by this man, and she only hoped he wouldn't let her down. She felt disappointed that Betty had not taken up with that John Coombes. He had been to the house a few times, mainly to see her husband on hauliers' business. He ran his own lorry, and she thought he and Betty had looked the ideal couple; and from what she had seen he appeared keen on Betty. But it was not to be, apparently. Betty seemed to have fallen for this Terry fellow. Still, it had changed her daughter for the better, and she crossed her fingers that things might turn out all right. At least John was calling to take Betty to the party!

"You look great," enthused John when Betty emerged from the house.

He took her hand and led her to his car.

"Thank you, John. I appreciate you taking me to Manchester. I don't think I would have had the courage to go on my own," she said quietly.

Getting in the driver's seat, John gave Betty a sideways look and patted her hand. "I couldn't let you go there on your own," he said, and just stopped himself from adding that it wasn't the right place for a young girl anyway. Betty was looking so happy he didn't want to start an argument.

An hour later, John parked the car in the parking lot and helped Betty out from the passenger's seat.

They could hear beat music coming from the club, and as they approached the Pink Dahlia's neon lights suffused their faces with a soft shade of pink. Betty felt nervous, and John, feeling her hesitation, took her hand.

"You look beautiful," he whispered warmly.

She sensed something wasn't quite right. He knew about her feelings over Terry, and she wondered if he was disappointed about it. Still, she couldn't help her feelings. 'He'll get over it,' she thought.

The noise from the club's resident jazz band vied with the din from the customers. John pushed his way through to the crowded bar, still hanging on to Betty. One of the drivers was ordering drinks from a busty blonde in a red satin low-cut dress.

He turned and, seeing John and Betty, grinned. "Our lot is over there. We've managed to get a table," Sam said, pointing.

John gave a thumbs up, and turning to Betty, who was looking a little dazed, asked her what she wanted to drink.

"A ginger beer, please," she mouthed above the noise. Then, turning, she stared at the blonde barmaid. Tugging at John's sleeve, she whispered urgently in his ear, "I think that blonde is a man, John."

John turned to stare at the barmaid. "I know, Betty. If you look around you'll see they are all men, some in drag," he whispered back.

Betty looked aghast. Turning she looked keenly at some of the men and 'women' huddled round the bar, then put a hand to her mouth to stop herself from laughing.

Quickly paying for the drinks, John led the way through the throng and guided Betty towards the table where the drivers were sitting.

"Cor, Betty, you're a sight for sore eyes, isn't she, John?" shouted Garry. The only way they could converse was by shouting above the noise of the music and the revellers, many of whom were gyrating on the dance floor.

"I don't understand. Why are there all these men here? And where's Terry? I thought it was his party," Betty shouted, looking perplexed.

The drivers began to laugh.

"I think Terry's coming over now," Garry said.

Betty turned to see Terry, dressed in an open-necked pink shirt with tight silver-grey trousers, coming towards them, his arm round a tall, thin man with a mop of white hair and a matching moustache.

"Glad you could all make it," Terry called, bending over towards Betty and kissing her cheek. "I hope you haven't paid for those drinks – I told Rodney the drinks were free for my party."

"We didn't know where you were, Terry, so we just ordered. Don't worry about it, mate – we'll tell him on the next round," Sam shouted.

Terry turned to the man with the moustache. "I don't think you've met Ricky, my partner. Ricky, meet the gang I told you about."

Ricky smiled and raised a hand in greeting before placing his arm round Terry's waist.

"We're going on to the dance floor now, but don't forget to order whatever you want from the bar," Terry shouted as he turned away.

One or two of the drivers raised their arms in acknowledgement, smiling amiably, but two or three others stared open-mouthed as Terry and his partner took to the floor.

"Blimey, I never knew Terry was gay. He kept that under wraps, didn't he?" mouthed Sam.

"He never said anything, but I guessed as much," Garry replied, looking keenly at Betty.

Betty was gazing into her glass of ginger beer as her face turned crimson.

"I shouldn't have come, John," she whispered in his ear.

John stood up, helping Betty to her feet. "We suspected Terry was gay, but didn't want to let him down. Betty wasn't feeling well before we came, so I think we'll call it a night, guys."

The drivers looked up, and nodded.

"Sorry you're not too good, Betty. This isn't the place for you, anyway. I'm sure John will see you home all right," Garry shouted. "I'll tell Terry you've had to go, shall I?"

John nodded, and then helped Betty push through the throng of men. Out in the fresh air, Betty seemed to collapse against John's shoulder. He led her to the car and silently they got in.

"I've been a complete fool! I thought he was interested in me. . . ." Betty's voice trailed away.

John turned to look at her face, tears already beginning to course down her cheeks.

"Why didn't you tell me? You let me go through all that and never said a word," she retorted angrily, her voice breaking.

"I wasn't sure at first. Terry kept his private life pretty close to his chest, for some reason. When he said he was having a party at the Pink Dahlia, I twigged," John replied as he drove from the club car park.

"You could have told me then!" Betty retorted.

"I tried to, but you just got angry, so I decided to go along with it," John said.

They drove the rest of the way in silence. As they approached Betty's home, she suddenly giggled. John, startled, looked at her, and then relaxed when he realised she really was laughing.

"What's funny?" he asked, smiling at her sudden transformation.

"That blonde barmaid – she, he, had the biggest Adam's apple I've ever seen!" Betty chortled.

Although some of the drivers met up at the motorway services several times during the next few months, they only saw John once, and Betty not at all. Terry, too, seemed to have disappeared.

"I hear that Terry's transferred to Scotland," Sam said when the drivers met on the M6 one autumn day ten months after the Pink Dahlia party.

"That was one funny party he had! I would never have guessed he was gay. Can't understand why he didn't tell us, though. My younger brother, Pete, is gay," Sam said, shaking his head as he drank his mug of tea.

"I liked old Tel. I thought Betty was keen on him for a bit," Garry said. "But you never can tell."

Just then, the door opened and John Coombes appeared, closely followed by Betty.

"Well, speak of the Devil – look what the cat brought in!" called Garry as John and Betty both made their way to the food counter.

A couple of minutes later, John approached and sat down with a loaded breakfast plate, looking decidedly sheepish. He was followed by Betty, carrying a plate of eggs, bacon, baked beans, hash browns and black pudding. She was looking her old big self again.

"Hey, our Betty, eating for two again, are we?" joked Garry.

John held aloft Betty's hand, displaying a wedding ring. "Yes, she is. The baby's due next year," he replied as the two began to tuck into their breakfasts.

THE LAST CRUISE

She peered out at the heaving grey sea, sloshing against the side of the ship in the growing gloom, and turned away from the stateroom window with a shudder. It was blowing a storm out there. Not that it made any difference. She had been feeling sick since they left port, and even the flattering pink light above the dressing-table mirror did nothing to hide the sallow tinge of her skin. How she hated these cruises!

"I look like a grapefruit," she groaned aloud, grimacing at her reflection.

"A grapefruit shouldn't be taking this trip, especially when a peachy fruit like Deirdre Dodds is making heavy play for its husband." Beryl took great comfort from talking to herself. At least that way there was no fear of reprisals.

Thinking of reprisals, Jack's face suddenly loomed unbidden in her thoughts. He would be on his third whisky and soda by now in his favourite watering hole, the Jolly Tar's Bar. No doubt Deirdre and Donald would be there, too, laughing at his crude jokes. At least, Deirdre would be laughing, casting flirtatious and come-hither looks at Jack under heavily mascaraed eyelashes. The woman's common cackle caused Beryl to shudder inwardly. Even so, she reluctantly had to admit that Deirdre was good-looking in a flashy sort of way. The woman wore far too much make-up, of course, and her full lips, coated in bright vermilion, were certainly awe-inspiring. Those lips never failed to fascinate

– fulsome, pouting, sometimes a small gooey hole down which champagne cocktail cherries would disappear; often wide and cavernous from which a loud staccato laugh would erupt. The mouth vied with a cloudy mass of Barbie-doll hair which looked deceptively fine, but which in reality felt like stiff funfair candyfloss.

She knew without a doubt that Jack's recent fondness for cruising, their third this year, lay with the glamorous Deirdre.

They had met the Doddses the previous year on a cruise in the Caribbean, and since then the pair had accompanied them on every trip. Donald Dodds appeared an unassuming fellow, totally dominated by the brash Deirdre, who appeared to show him nothing but contempt at his efforts to please her. She wondered what he had seen in the brash, gaudily dressed American that had prompted him to marry her.

She could understand Jack, of course. He had always liked blondes. She patted her own brown hair, neatly permed in a tight set, with satisfaction. Jack had tried to get her to bleach her own hair when they were first married, but she refused. She would have none of that vain nonsense.

Jack had turned out to be both rough and uncouth, a bully who could turn his anger on his wife in a flash. She couldn't remember how many times she had had to cover the bruises on her arms after one of their encounters. It usually happened after one of his drunken sessions, and she found she wasn't strong enough to counter his attacks. Deirdre, however, seemed a perfect soulmate for him; and, for her part, Deirdre seemed totally smitten. By now, Jack had probably got his hand on Deirdre's knee under the table, as she noticed he had the previous evening. The embarrassment of this action, amongst so many over the years, had finally decided her. This would definitely be their last cruise.

The plan was simple. It would look like an accident. Jack always got drunk every night on these cruises and often decided to go up on deck late at night for some fresh air. She felt she only had to bide her time before the opportunity presented itself for her to push him over the side. She wished she could get rid of Deirdre at the same time, but felt that this might be stretching things a bit far. One accident at sea would be acceptable, but two accidents would certainly cause suspicion. She had to content herself with Jack's demise!

She felt sure that Deirdre was planning to leave Donald for Jack. She had seen the cash signs glittering in the greedy woman's eyes whenever she looked at him. Deirdre knew that Jack was a self-made millionaire as head of Dodds Elasticated Hose Suppliers. He had bragged about it often enough, much to Beryl's disgust. Poor Donald was in insurance and from what he said he found it a struggle to finance so many cruises, which his wife insisted on.

It would give her great satisfaction to see all Deirdre's hopes and dreams tip overboard along with Jack!

If it wasn't for the money, Deirdre could have him, and welcome. In private he was foul-mouthed and cruel, and she wondered how Deirdre would cope with his philandering ways. She knew he would soon grow tired of the loud-mouthed blonde and start to trawl around for fresh conquests, so she felt she was grudgingly doing Deirdre a favour by getting rid of him.

Apart from his fortune, there was also the insurance money. She and Jack had insured each other against accidental death some time ago for over £1 million. Jack was, despite his wealth, mean with money when it came to his wife. He paid for her clothes and things she needed, but she never had any money she could call her own to do what she wanted. The thought of all that money took her breath away.

"What the hell do you think you are playing at?" Jack's bellow shook her from her daydream.

He was standing in the doorway, swaying slightly, eyes bloodshot. He'd had a skinful, she thought.

"I'm sorry. Jack, but I don't feel well enough to go to the bar tonight. You know how sick I get on these trips."

"Like hell you do!" he snapped. "This boat has the best stabilisers in the line, and the tablets that quack McAddams gave you should have done the trick by now. They cost me enough." Without warning, he suddenly grabbed her arm viciously, his fingers digging into her plump flesh. "Come on, I'll get rid of that sickness once and for all! A dose of sea air will do you good."

"Please, Jack," she wailed. "There is a storm out there – we can't possibly go on deck now."

"Don't be stupid, woman. On a ship like this there's no problem. Deirdre wouldn't hesitate. She's twice the woman you are," he gritted.

Beryl just managed to grab a chiffon scarf to put round her throat, but no coat, before he dragged her out of the cabin, along the deserted corridor and up a flight of stairs.

The deck was deserted. A fierce gale was in progress, and as he propelled her along the slippery deck her protests were drowned out by the shrieking wind and the spray which was whipping over the ship's rail.

Dragging her to the side of the ship, Jack let go of her. A strong gust of wind suddenly snatched at the chiffon scarf she was wearing and swept it high into the air. Quickly she lunged sideways to try and retrieve it, and was just in time to see her husband, arms outstretched, sail past her. For a fleeting moment she saw the murderous rage on his face turn to terror. Then, arms flailing wildly, he lost his balance and wordlessly disappeared over the side. Peering over the rail, she stared with almost detached interest at the boiling foam below. Jack did not surface. She decided to wait a couple of minutes, and then started to scream.

Later that evening, after much questioning and activity, during which the ship had turned back to make a fruitless search, Beryl was the centre of much sympathetic attention in the Jolly Tar's Bar.

Sipping a restorative double brandy and soda, with an attentive Deirdre and Donald hovering over her, Beryl looked suitably upset. Deirdre had all the appearance of an inflatable doll that had just been punctured.

"Poor Jack, and only two days out of Southampton," she sobbed, seeing all that cash floating away in the ship's wake.

"Poor Beryl, you must be devastated," Donald sympathised, patting her shoulder.

Thinking of how it was nearly herself who had ended up in the briny, she managed to give a sorrowful smile. "Yes, I'll miss him. In fact, I don't think I'll ever be able to face a cruise again," she murmured, her seasickness evaporating even as she spoke.

FIREWORKS

Charlie Jessop sat at the edge of the bed and slowly put on his trousers. He looked back at Marlene, who appeared sound asleep on the pillows. He marvelled at how she could sleep so soundly. The silly cow was becoming a liability, he thought sourly. It was as if she wanted Jim to catch them at it. It was obvious she wanted out, and finding him here would be a good way for her to scarper.

He bent to pull on his socks, and glanced back at her again. Even in sleep her face was beginning to look tired and worn. She'd had Botox on her forehead recently and it had only made her look odd, with a permanently surprised expression on her face. The afternoon sun caught locks of her peroxide-blonde hair. Why didn't she have a proper job done? Her hair looked dry and over-bleached. Jessop sighed, and tied the laces on his expensive crocodile shoes. It was going to cost him a packet to get rid of her, even without June finding out. Thinking of June, a slow smile spread over his face. Ah, June, the woman he'd married twenty years ago. Well, she was no looker these days, and he'd been disappointed they had been unable to have children. Still, she was cheaper than a housekeeper, and even helped him with his paperwork sometimes, visiting the factory from time to time. Yes, he was in no mood to ditch June – not yet, anyway. The thought of all the money he would have to part with if they divorced made him break out in a cold sweat.

He rose and went over to the bedroom window. His Silver Cloud was parked at the end of the garden. The sun shone on the pristine bonnet, and his heart sang. It had taken him fifteen years to afford the Rolls-Royce, and it was his pride and joy. The pleasure he got from driving it was better than being with any woman. He thought of June again – timid June, who wouldn't say boo to a goose. She'd stopped the sex years ago. He hadn't minded as there were plenty more fish in the sea. It was her loss, he thought, and it wasn't as if she'd been any good at it, not like Marlene.

He looked back at the bed again in disgust. "Hey, you lazy cow, time to get out of the pit. I expect Jim will be home from work soon. It's four o'clock."

The woman yawned and opened her eyes. She stared at Jessop for a long moment, and stretched.

"You're leaving already, Charlie? Jim won't be back until six – he's working late tonight. We've still plenty of time for a quickie."

Jessop looked at her irritably. "He might just come back sooner, and I don't intend getting caught in his bedroom."

Marlene yawned and slipped into a pink fluffy negligee. "Getting caught never bothered you before," she taunted.

Charlie turned from the window, an angry frown on his face. "What does that mean? Do you think I want my head punched in by that stupid moron of a husband of yours?"

Marlene rose from the bed and put an arm round him. "That need never happen. We could just go away together – go abroad. You've said before you'd like to get away from that frigid bitch of a wife of yours."

Charlie shook her off angrily. "You must be effing mad, woman! June would take me to the cleaners! I'll decide when the time is right to leave, and now is not the right time. I've spent a packet recently on updating safety measures at the factory. It's going to take time to recoup, like."

Marlene pouted, and sat down heavily on the bed. Looking

down at her, Charlie wondered what he had ever seen in her. Not much, apparently. He'd have to come up with some plan to shake her off. It wouldn't be easy, but he knew she liked money. He'd string her along for a bit longer, then dump the old dog-face. As for June – his face set in a gloomy line. He'd have to think up a different way of dumping his wife. It was true he had thought of moving abroad, but he didn't intend taking either Marlene or June. There were plenty more fish in the sea, particularly bikini-clad ones in the south of France.

He turned to look once more at the Rolls. "Must be off, then. I'll call you when I can," he muttered. He moved to the door, not wanting to see the look of resigned disgust on Marlene's face.

"There are times, Charlie Jessop, when I think you only want me for my body," she called out.

'How right you are!' Charlie thought as he headed for the stairs.

Reaching the garden path he inhaled the fresh air appreciatively, feeling free at last.

The massive explosion knocked him off his feet and sent him hurtling against the front door. Bits of glass and metal rained down, and the front windows of the house were shattered. Charlie staggered to his feet, blood pouring from his head. For several moments silence reigned, the heavy thudding of his heart the only noise. Then he half crawled, half hobbled down the path, taking in the sight of the smouldering ruin that had been his pride and joy. Clouds of black smoke assaulted his eyes, and the smell of cordite caused him to choke as he stared at the wreck of his car.

"Bastard!" he hissed through clenched teeth, tears springing to his smoke-blackened eyes. "He's done it this time. I'll bloody fire him when I get back, then I'll kill him."

He could feel the bile rising in his mouth, and his legs had turned to rubber as he sank down on the path. The smoke was now accompanied by tongues of flame that rose from the interior of the wrecked car.

"Was that yours, mate?" A workman was running towards him.

Charlie stood up slowly. For the first time he saw people racing towards the car, attracted by the explosion. Employees from a nearby mill were grouped in doorways or hanging precariously from high windows in order to catch a glimpse of the carnage. Soon, in the distance he heard the clanging of a fire-engine bell, followed by the wailing of an ambulance siren.

"Was there anyone in there?" asked the workman, trying to peer through the smoke.

Charlie shook his head, unable to speak.

"The fire brigade's here now. There's an ambulance coming as well. Look, mate, I think you're hurt," the workman added.

"Charlie, Charlie, thank God you're alive," Marlene was screaming, running down the path towards him, still in her pink negligee. She threw her arms round him, sobbing.

"I think your husband is hurt. He's lucky he wasn't in the car when it went up," the workman said, eyeing Marlene with more than a little lust in his eyes.

"I'm not her husband," Charlie grated, shaking off her arm.

The workman looked at the two of them and hid a grin.

Charlie turned away, and slowly put a hand to his cheek. There was no pain, but he felt the wetness and realised he was bleeding. He looked down blankly at the blood on his hand. Marlene was looking at the car, open-mouthed, seeing it properly for the first time.

"I'd better scarper. I'm not going to get involved in this. I'll have a job explaining this to Jim as it is. What the hell's going on, Charlie?" Marlene spat, looking frightened. "Whatever it is, I don't want to know. Don't call round here again." With that she flounced back up the path and disappeared.

"You'd better sit down. You look as if you might pass out any moment." A young woman wearing a green overall had joined the workman.

"I think he's suffering from shock," she said, turning to the ambulance men who had arrived on the scene.

Foam from the fire tender was already dousing the flames in the car. Then two police officers arrived, walking slowly towards him almost casually, as if an explosion in Bartholomew Road was something that happened every day.

"You can leave this with us now, sir," one of the officers said heavily, turning towards the workman. "You'd better get your colleagues well away from the vicinity in case there's a second explosion. We don't want any accidents, do we?" He turned to Charlie, who was gazing into space. "Now, sir, is this, or was this, your car?" He produced a notebook from his breast pocket.

"Yes, it was," Charlie replied dully.

"Have you any idea how this happened?"

"It was a firework, officer," Charlie replied. There was a note of agitation in his voice.

The officer snapped his notebook shut.

"He's suffering from shock. We need a stretcher over here," he called.

Gently, Charlie was helped into the ambulance, wrapped in a blanket.

"Constable Bates will accompany you, sir. If you have anything to say, he'll be on hand to help. In the meantime, Bates, I'll get on to the explosives people. Could be a terrorist job. We won't know until the army gets here. I'll have to cordon off the area and keep the press away."

Bates nodded as he closed the ambulance doors.

Tucked between crisp white sheets at the county hospital, Charlie felt suddenly tired. Just a short rest, he thought, and then he could sort it all out. . . .

Several hours later he woke, a vile taste in his mouth and a giant-sized headache.

"Mr Jessop?" A heavily built man in a dark suit was bending over him.

"How long have you been here?" Charlie asked testily.

"I'm Special Branch. You've been very lucky – just a few scratches and bruises. If you'd been in or nearer the car you would have been killed," he explained.

"How long do I have to stay in this bloody bed? I'm all right."

Charlie swept the covers aside and placed his bare feet on the cold lino. The room swam.

"Better take it easy, Mr Jessop. We've examined what's left of your car – Silver Cloud, registration number 890 JES." He was consulting his notebook.

"Yes. Where is it now? I'll have to get the insurance company on to it right away. I don't know how I'll be placed over this." Charlie closed his eyes.

"Well, we've examined the vehicle, Mr Jessop, and we've definitely established that it was not the work of any terrorist organisation."

If the man was expecting any sign of relief from Charlie, he didn't get it.

"Of course it wasn't bloody terrorists. I knew that from the start – in fact, I told that ruddy copper what caused the explosion," Charlie retorted.

"Oh, then you do have an idea on what caused the devastation, then?" The Special Branch officer leaned forward, intent on recording every word.

"I've already told them – it was a firework," Charlie said angrily.

"A firework!" The man looked amused.

"Yes, a firework. Look, if you'd done your job properly you'd have known I invent fireworks for the export market – giant rockets, huge firecrackers, that kind of thing. My factory is well known for it. I was carrying a box of a new prototype on the back seat – yes, I know it's illegal, but I had a deadline to meet. It's that stupid bloody manager, Jack Deacon. He'll get the sack this time. I told him to take more care when mixing the chemicals. I'd have been a goner if I hadn't decided to call, er, on a customer, before visiting the foreign client in Birmingham."

The detective sat back, a stunned look on his face.

"Do you mean to tell me that you believe one of your fireworks blew up your Rolls?" he asked incredulously. "Mr Jessop, your car was practically blown apart, as well as the damage it caused to surrounding properties."

Charlie lay back on the pillows, arms behind his head, a proud smile playing on his battered features. "Well, my new firework isn't called the Big Bang for nothing, mister."

"Oh, yes?" the man said, moving close to Charlie's smirking face. "Then tell me, Mr Jessop: how do you account for the remains of a bomb found under the chassis?"

The smile disappeared quickly from Charlie's face. "A bomb? Who? Why?" he stammered.

The man sat back in the chair. "We arrested Mrs June Jessop an hour ago – I believe she is your wife – along with your manager, Mr Jack Deacon, on suspicion of planting a bomb under your car. They are being charged with attempted murder."

"I don't get it," Charlie stammered. "June wouldn't do a thing like that – she wouldn't have the guts. Deacon I can believe, but not June."

The man laid a kindly hand on Charlie's shoulder. "I've been in this business for fifteen years, Mr Jessop, and I can assure you that anyone is capable of anything, given the right circumstances. They've both confessed. The thing is, your wife had insured you for over £2 million, and we found evidence that she and Deacon were planning to go away together."

"June and Jack Deacon?" Charlie croaked.

"I'm afraid so, Mr Jessop. Sorry you had to learn this just now, but you're on the mend, and no doubt they will be discharging you from hospital in the morning. I would get some rest now if I were you."

When the man had gone, Charlie lay back on the pillows, his

mind in a whirl. He closed his eyes, and after a few minutes a smile played on his bruised lips. Marlene had gone, and now June! Things could have turned out a lot worse, he thought. Now he wouldn't have to pay anything to get rid of them both. What a turn-up for the books! He sat up and looked out at the sunshine.

"South of France, here I come!" he chortled.

CUCKOO'S NEST

Muriel vigorously patted the soil around the winter pansy she'd just planted, aware that Sandra was watching from the sitting-room window. She gave the ground a final swipe with the trowel, wishing it was Sandra's head. She could almost hear what Sandra was saying to Brian. "Your mother shouldn't be out there at her age. We really must get a gardener."

Just another expense, following the cleaner they had to have because 'it's just too much for Muriel'.

"For goodness' sake, Brian, I might be a pensioner, but I'm not incapacitated. It's got to the stage when I can't do anything in my own home! I don't need a cleaner, and I like gardening," she'd fumed at her only son.

"Sandra is only doing what is best for you, Mother," Brian insisted. "You're not getting any younger, and you should be taking things easier. Sandra is only trying to help."

Muriel knew better. Sandra had taken over completely, even doing the shopping and deciding what Muriel should and should not eat.

"I do like kippers," she'd stated dejectedly, as Sandra dished up her own version of an organic fish pie.

"Come, come, Mother, they smell the place out for days, and you know I have my bridge club members coming round tonight," Sandra said dismissively.

That was another thing. Sandra's bridge club members were a

snobbish lot, self-opinionated, and had been more than a little patronising when they met her. Muriel had gone quietly to her room and left them to it. The sound of their shrill laughter could be heard through the ceiling. Reading a book had become almost impossible.

How she wished she had never invited her son and his wife to move in! The trouble was, Brian had lost his job in the recession, and the rent on their luxuriously appointed flat had gone up, making it impossible for them to make ends meet. Sandra had also stopped work when they married, and Muriel had been bitterly disappointed when Sandra informed her there would be no children.

"Brian and I discussed having a family when we married, and I made it quite clear that I didn't want children," Sandra had told her.

"What about Brian?" Muriel had asked. "Doesn't he want children either?"

"Well, if he hadn't felt the same way as me, I wouldn't have married him," Sandra replied with a grim smile.

Muriel was saddened at the prospect of no grandchildren. She knew Brian liked children and before meeting Sandra he had often spoken about having them one day. But she realised that where Sandra was concerned he was weak, and now it seemed it was too late.

Sandra and Brian had now settled happily in her home; and although Brian had now managed to get a lucrative position with an accountancy firm, it appeared the pair had no intention of moving into a place of their own.

She'd broached the subject of them finding somewhere else to live, but Brian had dismissed the idea.

"There's hardly any point in our moving now, Mother. The house will eventually he mine, and Sandra can help run the place. It's getting too much for you."

Muriel knew those words were Sandra's. The house wasn't

particularly large and was no trouble to run. In fact, it was easier for her now since the death of Edward, Brian's father, who had suffered a stroke while still in his fifties. She'd cared for him in those final years, and after his death had been contemplating what to do next when Brian's financial situation landed in her lap. Her sister, Janet, was also a widow living on her own. She had toyed with the idea of inviting her to come and live with her. They had always got on, sharing the same sense of humour, and Janet was fun to be with. Now all that seemed impossible.

She sighed, shaking the soil from her gardening gloves. Looking back at the house, she could still see Sandra in the bay window. She suddenly felt the urge to make a rude sign, but then thought better of it. "Janet wouldn't have given a second thought to doing that," she chuckled to herself.

Back in the house, Sandra watched her mother-in-law as she walked up the path.

"Really, Brian, there are times when I think your mother is going gaga," she retorted, turning to look at her husband, who was reading the morning paper.

"Oh, yes, dear." Brian, engrossed in the financial section, was not paying attention.

Sandra strode across and snatched the paper from her bemused spouse. "You're not listening, Brian. I think your mother is getting dementia. She sometimes mumbles to herself, and just now she's walking up the path smiling, and there's no one there!"

Brian stood and looked out of the window.

"She looks all right to me. She's probably smiling at some recollection. We all do it," he retorted, smarting at having his Saturday-morning read interrupted.

"That's the trouble with you, Brian," Sandra countered angrily. "Everything is all right, even when trouble is staring you in the face!"

Brian sighed heavily and returned to his chair. Sandra was always on about his mother's mental state. Perhaps there was something in it after all and he'd just missed it. His mother had always seemed a well-adjusted woman with a great sense of humour, but lately he'd noticed she didn't smile so much, and at times was downright tetchy. He suspected Sandra might have something to do with it, but didn't dare say so.

"What do you suggest we do?" he said finally.

"If your mother is starting to get confused, then I can't see how we can look after her here."

"You mean, put her in a home?" Brian sounded shocked.

"What alternative would we have? You know perfectly well, Brian, that I am not very strong. I take after my mother with my bad nerves and thinning bones," she said plaintively. "I couldn't possibly look after your mother here, and as you're working you certainly couldn't." Realising that Muriel might well be in the hall by now and able to overhear the conversation, she dropped her voice to an urgent whisper. "You'll have to look on the Internet and get some retirement-home brochures."

Muriel dropped her gardening gloves on the hall table and entered the sitting room. She knew by the uncomfortable atmosphere and the sheepish look on Brian's face that they had been talking about her.

"I'm all for a cup of tea. Anyone care to join me?" she asked calmly, going through into the kitchen.

"That's all right, Mother, I'll do it," Sandra retorted, bustling in and practically pushing Muriel away from the kettle.

"I'm perfectly capable of making a cup of tea in my own kitchen, Sandra," Muriel gritted, snatching the kettle from Sandra's grasp.

Sandra froze, looking shocked, and stood back, her neck turning a blotchy red.

"Well, really, there's no need to take that attitude, Mother. I was only trying to help."

"I don't need any help. I'm not without arms, and I wish you wouldn't treat me like a complete nitwit, Sandra," Muriel said heatedly.

Hearing the raised voices, Brian popped his head round the door. "What's going on?" He looked at his wife.

Sandra brushed past him. "Don't ask."

Brian followed her into the sitting room. "What was all that about?"

"Your mother has definitely lost it," she hissed. "I thought she was going to hit me with the kettle."

"Surely not," Brian said mildly.

"I'm telling you, Brian, she is becoming a danger to us as well as to herself. We've got to do something now and not wait until she burns the house down. While you were at work the other day I managed to get some brochures from retirement homes not far from here. They're upstairs in the bedside cabinet. Go and get them," Sandra instructed.

Reluctantly, Brian mounted the stairs with mixed emotions. He felt angry at Sandra's duplicity. He felt she was going over the top a bit. There were times when he felt he could hit her himself, but instead he hid away behind the newspaper. It was easier during the week. He looked forward to getting back to work, to the peace and order of his office, away from a wife who always seemed to be demanding something. It was a great shame she hadn't wanted children. They at least would have been a distraction. But there again they might have borne the brunt of Sandra's sharp tongue, or, even worse, turned out like her! As he searched the drawer for the brochures, he mused how different his life could have been.

Sandra's voice cut through his reverie. "Brian, what are you doing? Haven't you found them yet?"

"No, dear – still looking," he called.

A few seconds later she was there beside him, grabbing a couple of glossy colourful brochures.

"This is the one I was telling you about. It looks very promising." She closed the bedroom door, not wanting Muriel, who was making the tea, to overhear the conversation. "They allow you to have a few pieces of your own furniture to make you feel more at home. It would be ideal. Muriel could take that chest your father held so much store by. She seems attached to it, and we won't have much room for it here. She could also take some of her bedroom furniture. We could buy new for here. I've seen some lovely modern pieces in Potter's in the High Street." Sandra prattled away, ignoring Brian's obvious discomfort.

"I'm not sure Mother is going to go along with this," he muttered.

"Nonsense! I'm sure she'll love it, mixing with people her own age," Sandra said briskly, closing the brochure. "I think we should at least go and look at the place. When she sees how nice it is, I'm sure your mother will agree. If not, then you must persuade her it's for the best."

A couple of days later, Sandra and Brian drove up to the iron gates of Sunset Retirement Home, spelled out in large gold letters on the board by the walled garden. In smaller text it read, 'Those with Special Needs Catered for – 24-Hour Nursing'.

"Hmm, this may be just the place," Sandra enthused, seeing the converted stone manor house. A gardener was busy hoeing a giant flower bed of multicoloured pansies, set within a circular drive. "There, Brian, your mother's favourite flower. It's a good omen. She's sure to feel more at home when she sees them," Sandra said optimistically, sensing Brian's reluctance. She knew she had to do something to get Brian's co-operation. He'd been dragging his feet this last day or two, and she felt that unless she got things in motion he might change his mind altogether. So far, he hadn't said anything to his mother, and that was both worrying and irritating.

They were soon ushered into the office, a large sunny room

overlooking the front driveway. Mrs Jackie Bowen, who ran the place, rose to greet them from behind a large pine desk. A kindly-faced woman with faded brown hair framing a lightly lined face, she offered them coffee.

"No, thank you," Sandra replied quickly. "We can't leave Brian's mother for long. You never know what she will get up to."

Mrs Bowen showed concern. "Your mother suffers from Alzheimer's?" Her gaze was directed at Brian.

Brian looked uncomfortable. Mrs Bowen noted that so far his wife had done the talking.

Brian opened his mouth to speak, but was beaten to it by Sandra, who leaned forward as if what she was about to say was strictly confidential. "We feel that my mother-in-law is in the early stages of dementia. She certainly isn't normal. She talks to herself and is becoming quite aggressive."

"I see." Mrs Bowen sat back in her chair and looked at Brian. "Has she been seen by her doctor over this?"

This time Brian found his voice. "I don't think my mother suffers from dementia. She gets irritable at times; but then, who doesn't?" He looked pointedly at his wife.

Mrs Bowen felt she was getting the picture – one that she was all too familiar with.

"Your mother lives with you at the moment?"

"No, we actually live with her." Brian was looking distinctly embarrassed at the way the conversation was going.

"I see." Mrs Bowen was looking thoughtful. "But your mother feels she would be happier living in this sort of environment, with people her own age around her?"

Sandra looked relieved, feeling that the woman had thrown her a lifeline.

"Precisely," she said firmly, beginning to relax.

"I – I'm not too sure about that," Brian said lamely.

"Look, why don't you both have a look round, and if you

think it is a suitable placement for your mother, then perhaps she could come along and see the place for herself. After all, the decision will have to be hers."

Mrs Bowen rose and ushered them from the room. They followed her along a sunlit carpeted corridor until they came to a large sitting room. Several elderly people were sitting around, several of them asleep, others trying to watch a quiz programme on the large television. A young foreign-looking girl in a green apron was helping one elderly lady into a wheelchair.

"I'm just taking Mrs Markham to the toilet," the girl said.

"That's quite all right, Greta. I was going to ask you to show Mr and Mrs Stockwell round, but you carry on. I will do it."

For the next half-hour they were shown some of the ground-floor bedrooms, a large kitchen smelling strongly of fish, and a spacious dining room where each table was laid out for four people.

"It's much nicer if our residents sit in small groups for their meals. There is less confusion and they get on better," Mrs Bowen explained.

Brian remained silent during the tour, but Sandra seemed highly enthusiastic. "What a lovely place!" she exclaimed, turning to Brian. "I think your mother would be very happy here, Brian. It's ideal."

Although the retirement home seemed a pleasant-enough place, Brian was secretly horrified at the thought of his mother living there. He couldn't see her sitting in front of a television day after day surrounded by elderly people, half of whom seemed semi-comatose.

As they reached the front door, Brian turned to Mrs Bowen. "I really think we need to discuss this with my mother before we bring her here. I don't feel at all sure she will agree to leaving her home any time soon."

Mrs Bowen smiled. "I quite understand. If she is active and happy with her present surroundings, and does not have any serious health issues, then I'm sure she wouldn't find this suitable."

Sandra was unusually silent as they got in the car. Brian looked sideways at his wife s face, which was mottled red with suppressed anger.

"I don't know what you think you were doing back there," she seethed. "We won't be able to go there again. That woman obviously thinks we are trying to get rid of your mother and push her into a home."

"Yes, well, that is what it looks like," Brian countered mildly.

"I don't know what we're going to do. There is no way I am going to be able to look after your mother, not with my bad nerves, not to mention my thinning bones!" she said.

Brian sighed heavily. There had been no mention of these health problems when they married six years ago!

"Very well," he said finally, as they drove off. "We will talk things over with Mother – or at least I will. We are going to have to tread carefully. We'll look at a few more places first. Did you say you had other brochures?"

Sandra at last looked pleased and sat back happily for the rest of the journey.

"You haven't been that long." Muriel smiled as they entered the sitting room.

Seeing his mother sitting there so comfortably, Brian felt a stab of guilt. What was he thinking?

"We just did a bit of window-shopping seeing as how Brian had the day off. He needs a new overcoat," Sandra lied. "Brian, I'm just going upstairs." She looked meaningfully at her spouse.

Brian followed her into the hall.

She turned and whispered urgently, "While I'm up there, you'd better have a word about you-know-what with your mother."

"What, now?"

"Yes, now," she said firmly, and stomped determinedly up the stairs.

Brian's mouth felt dry, and on seeing his mother's face he felt she knew something was going on.

"We've been discussing the future this last day or two, Mother, and were wondering how we would manage as you got older and . . ." His voice trailed away.

"You mean if I started to go doolally, or suddenly found I couldn't walk!" she retorted. "Well, we were wondering how Sandra would cope."

"When the time is right, I'll do my own planning, thank you," Muriel replied briskly.

Brian opened his mouth to reply when there was a loud shriek, followed by something heavy bouncing down the stairs.

Mother and son stared at each other for a couple of shocked seconds.

"Sandra!" Brian exclaimed, and rushed from the room, closely followed by Muriel.

Sandra lay huddled at the bottom of the stairs, her right leg at a strange angle, blood pouring from a wound to her forehead.

"My God, Sandra, what have you done!" Brian cried, going to cradle his wife's head.

She was unconscious and obviously hadn't heard him. Muriel was already reaching for the hall phone.

"Whatever you do, don't move her, son," she instructed.

Muriel and Brian sat in silence in the waiting room of the accident and emergency section of the local hospital. Sandra hadn't gained consciousness when they had brought her in by ambulance, and now they had to wait.

Eventually, a doctor came out to see them, looking grave.

"Please, is my wife going to be all right?" Brian asked, his voice shaky.

"Well, she has concussion, but the head wound is only

minor. Unfortunately she suffered a compound fracture to her right leg, and this will take some considerable time to heal, bearing in mind that Mrs Stockwell suffers from some degree of osteoporosis."

"She said it runs in her family – thinning bones, I mean," Brian said feebly.

Muriel squeezed his hand comfortingly.

"Can we see her?" she asked.

"Of course. They are taking her up to the ward now."

"How long is she likely to be in here?" Brian asked.

The doctor sighed. "I'm not sure, but Mrs Stockwell will be unable to walk on that leg for some time."

Brian looked shocked, and Muriel managed to get him back on to the seat.

"Now you have to be brave, son. You don't want Sandra to see you in such a state," she remonstrated, feeling like she was talking to the child he once was.

A month later, and Muriel was getting ready to visit her daughter-in-law when the front doorbell chimed. Opening the door, she was met by the laughing face of her sister Janet.

"I thought I'd give you a bit of support today!" she exclaimed. "How is the patient?"

Muriel rolled her eyes. "Don't mention it. I feel I have to go when Brian is working, but to be honest I feel really depressed when I leave her. She's not the best of patients."

"When is she expected to come out of hospital?" Janet asked as they made their way to her car.

"I honestly don't know. It was a shocking break and at one stage they were talking of amputation. Her bones are really brittle, apparently. There is talk of sending her to a convalescent home later. She will need a lot of physiotherapy, too, if she is ever to walk properly again. Brian is naturally devastated."

"How on earth did it happen, Muriel?"

"Brian blames those blessed high heels she was always wearing, but Sandra blames me," Muriel answered grimly.

"Blames you?" Janet repeated, steering the car out of the driveway. "Well, that's rich, I must say."

Muriel sighed. "She'd gone upstairs to get some brochures. I later found out they were for retirement homes for me! They were scattered all over the stairs. I think she thought I would be better off living with people my own age."

Janet snorted in disgust. "What she really wanted was you out of the way so she could play lady of the manor. I could see that coming."

Muriel sighed and gazed out of the window. "I don't think Brian would have allowed that," she said quietly.

"Maybe not, Muriel, but he's always been a bit soft where Sandra was concerned. Never likes to cause a scene. Anyway, I have a plan which might suit all of us in the long run," she grinned. "Well, almost all of us!"

Muriel looked at her sister's mischievous profile. "What is this great plan, then?"

"Wait and see! I'll explain everything when we get there. I phoned Brian and he promised to get out of work early to be at the hospital."

Janet parked the car, and together the sisters walked swiftly through the hospital entrance.

Sandra was sitting out of bed in an armchair, with her leg propped up and heavily bandaged. Brian was already there, holding her hand.

Sandra frowned at the two women as Brian rose to greet his mother and his aunt.

"How nice to see you, Janet," Sandra said frostily. "I suppose you are another one come to tell me off for wearing high heels!"

"Not at all, Sandra," Janet said smoothly, kissing the patient's cheek. "In fact, as I said to Brian over the phone, I have come up with a perfect solution to your problem."

"You've found a way of getting me a new leg, then," Sandra replied sarcastically.

Janet smiled. "Not exactly. I think you both know that you won't be able to return to Muriel's house. The ground floor isn't big enough to accommodate a bedroom, and you would never manage those stairs again. Sandra. So, I have suggested to Brian, and he is very happy with the plan, that we swap homes! You can rent my little bungalow, and I can move into the house! It's what we had planned before you and Brian moved in. Muriel and I between us could manage the house quite well."

"It really is the perfect solution, Sandra," Brian enthused, squeezing his wife's hand.

Sandra looked shocked, remembering Janet's tiny bungalow with some distaste. She opened her mouth to speak, but no words came out. She realised suddenly that she would never be in a fit state to object; and, looking at the three smiling faces in front of her, she realised she was outnumbered, and defeated.

THE HAYSTACK MAN

"Suleimanieh is not far now." The excited shout from his Kurdish driver tipped James Collins from a light doze into sudden awareness.

Through a blur of dust and sweat he peered out at the flat greyish-brown landscape broken by the outline of foothills to his left. The terrain hadn't changed much since they left Erbil the day before.

"How the hell do you know where we are?" he growled, shifting uncomfortably on his seat. He was tired to the bone, and nothing had prepared him for this searing heat and the sharp cold at night. The weariness and discomfort went hand in hand with the fear that had clawed at his stomach since they crossed the border.

"You see, Mr Collins. Not far," the driver assured him.

The vehicle bucked and swung like a wild horse, and Collins hung on grimly, sliding around the worn seat in his own sweat.

Collins turned to look at the elated profile of the little Kurd and marvelled. Shirin had appeared at his Istanbul hotel ten days before, offering Collins his services as driver and interpreter. Collins, who had been deciding on giving up his attempt to enter Iraq, had snatched at the offer, particularly as the Kurd had been confident he could get him across the border. So far he hadn't regretted his decision to go on. Shirin's cunning had enabled them to cross the mountains unscathed. They had come across a motley trail of mixed traffic on the journey – beaten up old trucks carrying dangerously secured drums of petrol, as well as people on foot leading herds of moth-eaten-looking goats. But they had only encountered aircraft from a distance as they crossed the border, surprisingly unhindered, and Collins more than once wondered at their amazing luck. He'd expected some officials or even soldiers at checkpoints, but it had all seemed chaotic; and although they were eyed with suspicion by people travelling the other way, no one seemed interested enough to stop them.

Twice the flat green bellies of large military helicopters had suddenly dropped down on them, hovering like giant greenfly in great swirls of dust.

Shirin had grinned then at the alarm on his companion's face.

"Don't be afraid, Mr Collins. Americans. We OK so long as we stay north of the 36th parallel." The Kurd seemed to have an astounding knowledge, and an almost childlike confidence in the so-called 'safe haven' provided by the allies.

Collins took a swig from his water bottle and almost gagged on the warm fluid. He wiped the neck and passed it over to the driver, who drank greedily without taking his eyes off the rough highway.

Rubbing a dirty hand across the grey stubble of his chin, Collins wondered if he would find Jonathan in Suleimanieh. He doubted it now. It would be too easy, and nothing about Jonathan had ever been easy.

Even as a child, his only son had been consumed with the wanderlust, an adventurer that the family could not understand or make any sense of. Twice he had run away from school, the first time managing to get as far as Dublin after stowing away on an Irish ferry.

Over the years, Collins had tried to put himself in his son's shoes; tried to think like him in order to track him down. Once, Jonathan had been missing for eight months. He was only twelve then. Collins had eventually traced him to London, despite the doubts of family and friends that he would be able to do so.

"You'll never find him, old man. It's like looking for a needle in a haystack there. Let him come home under his own steam," his brother had advised.

But Maude, his wife, had been beside herself with grief and worry. "James is very good at finding this particular needle," she had replied quietly, confident that her husband would find their son.

Surprisingly, after the London escapade Jonathan had settled down to his studies and eventually gained a teaching diploma. Maude had been very proud of him.

Thinking of Maude, Collins was suddenly swamped by the pain of his loss.

"He's not dead, James, no matter what they say. I just feel he is still alive, and you'll find him, I know you will," she'd whispered. That was three months ago. The confidence she had instilled in him before her death had strengthened his determination to come to Iraq and trace his son once again.

"Out of the question, Mr Collins," the assistant to the British consul had told him when he approached their offices in Istanbul.

The official leafed through a thin file as he sat behind a heavy, ornate desk. Collins watched the man's hands as he picked over the papers – slim, pale hands with long tapered fingers that Collins felt should belong to a woman. The silence had been almost tangible, broken only by the soft whirr of a ceiling fan.

"I believe the Foreign Office have already informed you of your son's death, have they not?" The official looked up then.

"Yes," Collins admitted warily, dropping his gaze to his own hands, which had been tightly clenched since he entered the room. "But I don't believe Jonathan is dead, and my late wife didn't think so either. Fair enough, we haven't heard from him in over a year, and Maude's illness happened too quickly for our son to be informed. He's always going off on some crusade or other. But above all he's a survivor. I just know he is alive somewhere out there."

The official was looking at him pityingly before he transferred his gaze to the notes in front of him.

"It says here that you are a technical adviser in the oil industry."

"I left soon after my wife's death. I took early retirement," Collins replied tersely. "I wound up my affairs in England, and came out here. I don't feel I have anything to lose."

The consular official rose from the desk. "Nothing to lose but your life, Mr Collins," he said quietly.

The two shook hands, and as Collins was about to leave, the man called out, "Oh, one final thing. Did you know your son was reported to be with the Peshmerga at the time the Iraqis came down heavily on the Kurds in the north, just after the Gulf War?"

"So I was informed," Collins replied. "But my son came to Iraq to teach. He isn't a soldier."

The man raised an eyebrow. "Well, good luck, Mr Collins. You'll need it. But I must advise you strongly against trying to enter Iraq illegally. You could be charged with spying, or simply disappear – who knows?"

Well, thought Collins, so far he had been lucky, thanks to Shirin. He glanced once more at the little driver, who was now whistling tunelessly through cracked lips.

Collins was about to say something, when there was a sudden explosion, and the road in front of the vehicle rose up like a brown monster, spewing dust and flame. He heard Shirin scream as he applied the brakes, but it was too late. The Land Rover lurched sideways. Collins felt the air being sucked from his body as he was tossed about like a pebble in a tin can. The vehicle rose, and then plunged downwards into a black void.

Collins woke to pain – a searing pain in his head and pain down his body. He tried to move, but his limbs felt too heavy. Carefully he opened his eyes. He was surrounded by what appeared to be dark-green canvas, and somewhere near he could hear a strange clicking noise. After several minutes lying there, he found he could raise his head, and he saw a square of open canvas, the hot sun streaming through. He realised he was in the back of a truck. The heat was oppressive, and he suddenly felt sick. He realised he badly needed water. He tried to lick his swollen lips, but his tongue was too dry, and above the clicking noise he now became aware of the insistent buzzing of flies. He tried to move his legs again, and this time succeeded. Painfully, he crawled to the opening and peered out.

Below him, only a few yards away, a group of bedraggled young children were kneeling in the dust, playing some sort of game, the stones they were throwing click-clicking as they played. About fifty yards away he saw a group of men, leaning against another truck, chatting. His heart sank as he saw the rifles slung casually across their shoulders. There was no doubt, he thought grimly, he had been caught by the Iraqis.

Just then, one of the men looked up, and, seeing Collins at the entrance to the truck, sauntered across, a smile on his bearded face.

"Ah, Mr Collins, you have come round. Perhaps a little drink will make you feel better." The man offered Collins a can which felt surprisingly cold.

Collins looked down at the can of Coke in bewilderment.

"You've had a lucky escape. First, your driver was five miles south of the safe zone. We believe he was actually taking you to Baghdad. Luckily for you some Iraqi pilots can't tell the difference between Baathist spies and Kurds. They tried to bomb your Land Rover, but hit the road ahead. Your driver was killed. You just have a few cuts and bruises – nothing to worry about." The man flashed him a gold-toothed smile.

Collins drank deeply before he could manage to speak. His head was teeming with questions, but at least the pain was subsiding and he was relieved to realise that he had suffered no broken bones.

"Shirin told me we would hear about my son at Suleimanieh," he croaked.

"A lie, Mr Collins. Your son is dead – but then, I believe you have already been told that." The man cocked his head to one side, eyes glittering like black diamonds.

Ignoring this statement, Collins asked, "Who are you? You talk like an Englishman!"

The man extended a dark-brown hand. "Forgive my bad manners. I am Nasir. I was educated at your Oxford. I love England. Tell me, is Gooch still captain of the England cricket side?"

Collins smiled. "I believe he is, but I'm not interested in cricket. I came here to find my son."

Nasir sighed, and climbed into the truck. "Mr Collins, if I give you proof of your son's death, will you leave Iraq? I have already arranged for you to be picked up at first light tomorrow."

Collins' heart sank. He could only nod. It would appear that his journey this time had been for nothing.

A small convoy of three trucks and a Jeep followed them along the highway when they eventually set off after a meal of mutton and tomatoes. Just before nightfall they halted on the edge of what looked like a small town. There were signs that Kurds were trying to build their lives in piles of rubble, but there were more tents than complete houses. The police station stood at the edge of the community. It had been badly damaged, with doors hanging loose and peeling paint and debris everywhere. Nasir informed him that Kurds now lived in what had once been police cells.

They dismounted from the truck and entered the cool gloom of the main building. Their footsteps sounded hollow on the bare, dusty concrete. Nasir had brought a flashlight, and its thin beam picked out the peeling yellow-ochre walls of the small cells. Finally, he arrived at the last room. The light played on the far wall where several names and messages had been scrawled on the uneven surface. Pity welled within Collins at the sight. Here were the last words of young men whose last desperate act had been to scratch their names on the wall in the hope that one day someone would recognise their plight, and at least remember their names.

Neither man spoke as Nasir raised the torch higher and let it play on some words written there. Astounded, Collins saw that there were English words there. Aloud, he read the message: 'My name is Jonathan Collins, born January 25th 1960. They hang us today, March 22 1991. God help us.'

There was silence as Collins digested the message, then wordlessly he turned away and swiftly walked out of that dreadful place into the heat of the late afternoon.

Nasir placed a sympathetic hand on his shoulder as Collins stood there, deep in thought.

I'm sorry you had to see that, Mr Collins, but I feel you would not have gone without wanting to do so."

Huddled in blankets, Collins watched the black speck appear over the horizon of a bitterly cold dawn. Nasir helped him down from the truck, and the two stood silently while the noise grew louder as the United Nations helicopter approached.

Suddenly Collins turned to his Iraqi companion. "Nasir, I don't know who you really are, but obviously you are a man of influence and importance. When you see my son again, will you please give him this and tell him to come home when he can." He handed over a small gold locket that had belonged to Maude.

For a moment, the two men gazed at each other, then the Iraqi freedom fighter threw back his head and roared with laughter.

"How did you know?" he managed at last.

Collins was shouting now above the roar of the aircraft. "My son and I had a code – a way of letting each of us know that we were OK. His was to give an incorrect birthdate. He is actually thirty-two. He was born on the 13th of March 1959."

Collins grinned then at Nasir's look of astonishment.

A minute later, aboard the helicopter, he imagined rather than heard Nasir's laughter as he settled back in his seat.

So, he hadn't traced his son this time, he thought. But perhaps the needle would find his own way home one day. He could only hope so.

GATEWAY TO THE STARS

"One thing we must remember: humans panic," Sowak announced.

There were several nods of agreement from the gathered assembly.

"We have all experienced that," Namod, one of the top space pilots, interjected.

"Only last Earth month I was surveying the big water beside the land these humans call America, when I was almost intercepted by several of their air machines. They are getting faster, but still no match for us. I was out of their vision within three seconds."

Sowak frowned. "These humans have been a worry since they left their planet and landed on that piece of planet debris they call Moon. They are now sending their machines further afield, and one day they will leave their solar system and invade ours."

Garon, one of the elders, looked worried. "Surely that is a long way off?"

"I think not," replied Sowak. "These humans are learning fast. It is only 100 or so of their Earth years since they discovered flight. Nothing will stop them now. They are inquisitive specimens, almost as adventurous as ourselves. They are straining to leave their planet to look for signs of life forms elsewhere. It is only a matter of time before they break through and discover that we, and others, exist."

"How long do you think it will be before they discover our planet system?" queried Namod.

Sowak pondered. "It is hard to say. These humans are aggressive. They constantly fight. The planet may look beautiful from a distance, but we must remember that these humans are gradually destroying their Earth. Not only that, but they kill one another, and also eat the next life form down the mammal chain. Some are even known to eat each other!"

Janus, one of the administrators, shuddered. "I don't like the sound of that – fighting and eating each other!"

Sowak smiled. "Do not concern yourself too much. As far as compassion goes, they have a long way to go yet. Because they are always at war, they remain poor, so they do not have the resources to move too quickly on to the next step. Remember, light centuries ago our kind were very similar in character to these humans. It is just that we progressed at a faster pace."

"If that is the case, then we should leave well alone," Janus retorted.

"We cannot do that." Sowak's voice had a worried edge to it, and the assembly turned to look at him expectantly. "There is a problem," he announced.

There was a tense silence in the room.

"Many of these humans are unstable. They could destroy themselves and their solar system quite easily."

"Come, come, Sowak! Isn't that an exaggeration? You said yourself they still had a long way to go, and because of their warlike nature progress is slow. How could they possibly destroy their planetary system?" Janus looked around the assembly for support and got it.

"Yes, Sowak, where could they possibly get the power to destroy their planet let alone their space environment?" asked Namod.

There were murmurs of agreement from the gathered elders.

Sowak held up a hand for silence. "The human capacity to destroy itself is immense," he intoned gravely. "Thanks to their aggressive nature these humans have invented instruments of mass destruction based on the very code of the life force itself. They can produce what they call 'bombs' which could ignite a chain of destruction they would be unable to stop. It could result in a massive explosion so great that it could not only destroy their planet but send destructive force waves rippling through the solar system. It could well have a knock-on effect with our own planetary system."

"This can't happen. What can we do?" It was the ever practical Namod. He was the top space pilot, always ready for action.

"Namod, so far we have only observed these humans from a distance. We have intercepted their air messages and watched their behavioural patterns from our spacecraft, but as yet we have not attempted to investigate the human mindset. We need to know more about the complex brain structure of these humans." Sowak was looking at a large map of the planet laid before him.

"What do you propose to do, Sowak?" asked Janus, slightly alarmed at the turn of events. "Surely you don't propose we go down there and start up a brain clinic. As you said before, these humans easily panic.

Sowak patted Janus on the shoulder reassuringly. "No, my friend, I do not propose to conduct any experiments on that terrible planet. These humans must come to us voluntarily."

"Oh, yes, I can just see several thousand humans rushing to be experimented on by those they would call aliens," sneered Namod.

"Well, what is your plan, Sowak? How can you possibly lift humans from their environment without causing panic? Also, how many are you hoping to abduct in order to carry out these experiments?" Janus sounded sceptical about the whole thing.

Sowak appeared unperturbed. “I think we will need several hundred, if not several thousand, to conduct our experiments properly.”

“Although I see the need for these experiments, Sowak, how long will they take and how will these humans fare afterwards?” This from Agart, an elder.

“As you know, my friends, these experiments need only take an hour or two, considering our vast medical knowledge. The human brain is apparently far less complex than our own, although we have still much to learn from it, and I am assured that these humans will be returned to their environment without being aware that they have ever left.”

“But how are you going to get them away without causing panic in the first place?” persisted Namod.

Sowak smiled. “These humans won’t even know they are entering our spacecraft. Not only that, but they will go through the entrances without a murmur, even eagerly, I promise you.”

True to his word, an Earth week later, several spacecraft entered the Earth’s atmosphere and landed at strategic points around the world.

Each spacecraft was decked out in bright lights at its entrance, and above each opening in red and yellow neon was emblazoned the word ‘McDonald’s’.

BLITZED

“Betty’s coming with the little ’uns.”

Jesse looked up from the fatless sponge she was mixing and stared at her husband. “Oh, yes, and how long is she staying?” Jesse made the question sound more like a threat.

Tommy senior looked up, sensing the anger emanating from his wife. She never read any letters that came to the house, always leaving them for Tommy to read and deal with.

“Tomorrow,” he said shortly, waiting for the storm.

“Tomorrow? I can’t get everything ready by tomorrow. You know what those kids are like – into everything. I’ll have to move all my best china out of the back room. Why does she have to come here, and now?” Jesse’s voice rose a couple of octaves as she banged the wooden spoon into the cake mixture.

“Now, now, Jesse,” Tommy said soothingly, tapping his pipe against the hearth, at the same time wishing he was tapping it against the side of his wife’s head.

“You know as well as I do that they can’t stay in London much longer – too dangerous. And we did promise our Tommy that we would look after them if things got bad.”

“Well, Betty’s managed so far, and why can’t she go to her mother’s in Great Yarmouth? Why do we have to take it on?”

“Because we promised Tommy, that’s why. Betty must be at the end of her tether with the nightly bombings. Our Tommy would never forgive us if we turned them away.”

Jesse sniffed and flounced from the room. "Better get some sheets for the spare bed, then. They'll all have to sleep in Tommy's old room," she said as she slammed the door.

Tommy sighed. He could never understand why his wife disliked their daughter-in-law. She was a nice woman, and she was bringing up the kiddies well while young Tommy was doing his bit for the war. Tommy was their only child, and he felt that there was perhaps a bit of jealousy there where his wife was concerned. When the young 'uns came along, he thought Jesse might have softened her attitude, but if anything she was worse. The last time Betty visited with the children, Jesse had kept them in the kitchen, explaining to Tommy later that she was worried the children might smash her porcelain figures which she kept on shelves in the back parlour. Well, there was no doubting that Jesse was house-proud, he thought ruefully.

She'd put an old carpet on top of her 'best' one in the parlour, for fear of getting it dirty or damaged, and he always had to take his shoes off when he entered the front door, after spending a minute or two wiping his feet on one mat at the step, and another one just inside the hallway. The parlour was definitely out of bounds, particularly when he was smoking his pipe. The use of the posh room was for Sundays only, or when they had important visitors, or friends Jesse was determined to impress.

Tommy sighed and looked at the clock. Time he was making a move. He was due for a meeting at the church hall with members of the Home Guard.

"Jesse, I'm off. See you later," he called as he laced up his boots by the front door.

Betty climbed down from the train, pulling the pushchair housing little Lily after her. Young Tommy was next, helped by a kindly porter who carried the small suitcase on to the platform. She looked anxiously around, hoping that Grandpa Tommy hadn't forgotten they were coming today. It had been a bit of a short notice, but after that last air raid the night before she knew she had to get away from the Elephant and Castle as soon as possible. She hadn't been able to let Tommy, her husband, know what she was doing. She knew he was somewhere in North Africa with the army, but she hadn't heard from him for over a month. Her neighbour, Daisy, had had a telegram to say her own husband had been injured, but there had been no details, and Betty dreaded the thought that a telegraph boy would ride up to her door with a similar yellow envelope.

She suddenly caught sight of the old man at the far end of the platform, and waved enthusiastically. She loved Grandpa Tommy, as did the children. Grandma Jesse was another story. Betty's face clouded at the thought of having to stay at Tommy's parents' house. The old lady was fussy and didn't like the children going into any room except the kitchen. Betty knew she would have to keep a close eye on them so as not to upset Jesse. She just hoped she would be able to find somewhere else to live close by before too long.

"Hello, love. Had a good journey?" Tommy kissed her warmly and turned to his grandchildren, giving Tommy a hug and patting Lily on the top of her fair hair.

"They were so excited about coming to stay, and they loved it on the train," Betty said, placing little Tommy close to the pushchair. Grandpa Tommy picked up the suitcase and they moved out of the station.

"You haven't got much here for the three of you," he commented.

"We had to leave a lot of our things in the house," Betty admitted. "The children wanted to take some toys, but there was no way I could carry more than the essentials."

"Well, I'm sure we can find something for them to play with, and then there's the park," Grandpa Tommy said encouragingly.

But if truth be known he was feeling apprehensive about Jesse. He knew she wouldn't like having the grandchildren around, and he felt sorry for Betty. Life wasn't going to be easy from now on.

Jesse was standing at the door, arms folded, as the little group arrived at the house.

"Nice to see you, Betty, but I'm surprised you wanted to come here," Jesse stated shortly, giving her daughter-in-law a quick peck on the cheek. She turned to the children and gave a tight smile. "Well, young Tommy, haven't you grown?" she said, ruffling his hair. "Lily looks like she might be walking soon, too." She stood aside to let them enter the kitchen, then put an arm on Betty's shoulder. "Take off your shoes when coming in, and that goes for young Tommy, too," she said abruptly.

"Nay, Jesse, give 'em a chance to get their breath," Grandpa Tommy protested.

"It's all right for you, Tom, but it's me that has to clean the house, and it's not easy," she answered, glowering at her husband.

Betty looked nervously at the two of them, and quickly removed her shoes, at the same time grabbing young Tommy.

"Take your shoes off in the house," she ordered him quietly. "You don't want to make a mess on Granny's carpet."

Young Tommy quickly pulled off his shoes without undoing the laces, and looked fearfully at Grandma Jesse. "My shoes aren't dirty, Mum. Why have I to take them off inside?" he complained.

"There's always dirt under shoes, and you take them off while you stay here," Grandma Jesse said sternly.

They all moved into the kitchen, and Grandpa Tommy was relieved to note that Jesse had made some effort to make the little family welcome. There was a cottage pie steaming on the table.

"You must be hungry after the journey. It isn't much, and I had to queue for over an hour at the butcher's when I got news they had beef mince. But I need your ration books, mind, as I can't feed you all on what we get. There is little enough as it is."

Betty nodded, and quickly removed her coat. "Tommy sits well at the table, now, Grandma Jesse, but I'll have to feed baby Lily on my knee, if you don't mind."

Jesse nodded, and began to serve up the food. "After supper I'll show you to your room. You'll all have to share a bed. Tomorrow I'll borrow a cot from my neighbour, Doris, but there won't be much room. It's a small bedroom that our Tommy slept in before he joined the army."

"I don't mind sharing with the children," Betty said gratefully. "I'm just happy to be here. We'll all feel a lot safer now. I can't remember when I last had a good night's sleep."

Grandpa Tommy patted her hand sympathetically. "Our Tommy will be relieved that you've come here, love. London is no place for the little 'uns right now."

"I don't know why you came here, though. What about your mother in Great Yarmouth? I'd have thought you'd want to go there," Grandma Jesse said, carefully placing a forkful of mince and potato into her mouth.

Betty looked down at her hands, knotted together nervously. "Mum has had to move in with my Aunt Hilda. She's not well. I would have liked to have taken care of her, but there wasn't room for all of us."

"Well, there's not much room here, either. I've got a lot of china in the parlour, and it isn't suitable for children," Jesse said shortly.

Tommy gave her a pained look. "Our Tommy will be glad they came here. We can always sort something out for them later."

"I'll make sure little Tommy doesn't go into the parlour, Grandma Jesse," Betty assured her, mentally crossing her fingers. She knew Tommy was at that lively stage when an out-of-bounds room didn't mean anything.

After the meal Jesse climbed the stairs and showed them to her son's old room. There was a small bed with a patchwork quilt, a bedside table and a small lamp. A narrow wooden wardrobe stood in the corner, with a hard-backed chair next to it.

"This'll have to do," she said. "The bed's only small, but you'll have to manage until tomorrow. You should have let me know a bit sooner that you were coming."

The old lady left Betty and the children alone and stomped down the wooden stairs. Holding the little ones close, she looked round the little room and felt chilled. The fact that it had once been Tommy's room did nothing to comfort her. The bedroom had not been used for some time and there was a slightly damp, neglected air about the place. She shivered and then turned to little Tommy, who had been silent for some time.

"Don't you mind, love, everything will be all right. At least we're safe here," she whispered, holding him close.

Lily was lucky, she thought, looking at her baby, who had fallen asleep as soon as she placed her on the bed. It had been a long day and they were all exhausted.

The following morning they trooped down to breakfast, and Betty was aware of the tension in the air as soon as she entered the little kitchen.

Grandpa Tommy looked up as they entered and smiled broadly. "Did you have a good night, love?" he asked.

"Not really," Betty answered ruefully. "Lily woke up about three and I couldn't get her to sleep again. It's being in strange surroundings, and then she's not used to sleeping with little Tommy and me. It was a bit of a squeeze."

Grandma Jesse doled out porridge to each of them without saying a word.

"I'm sorry, but did we wake you up?" Betty asked her, looking anxious.

"Aye, you did, and I didn't get a wink after all that noise," the old woman said tersely.

"We'll get a cot for Lily," old Tommy said reassuringly.

Little Tommy looked from one to the other, but stayed silent. He didn't like it here. There were no toys to play with and he had an idea he wouldn't be allowed to play in the street. He missed his friends already. Lily started to howl. Apparently, she didn't like it here either.

"After you've finished, get the children's things and go down to the park. I need to clean round here and I can't do so with you all under my feet. I don't expect you back until dinner time at twelve thirty," Jesse said.

Carrying the baby, Betty mounted the stairs to get the children's coats. She sat on the bed and put the baby's coat and shawl under her arm. Just then she heard raised voices.

"You naughty boy. What did I say? You're not to go into this room, and you're not to touch my china. Put that shepherdess down before you break it, and get out." It was Jesse, who sounded furious.

Betty poked her head round the parlour door, and saw little Tommy standing there holding a delicate china shepherdess and looking tearful.

Jesse snatched the statue from his hand and turned to Betty. "I told him not to come in here. I won't have him running riot in my house. If you want to stay here you'll have to keep him under control!"

"I only wanted to look at the things, Mum. I didn't mean no harm," Tommy said, beginning to cry as he turned to his mother.

Betty ran over and hugged him. "I know you didn't, love, but these are Grandma's precious things and she doesn't like people coming in here without her say-so."

Still looking like thunder, Jesse turned and marched out of the room, closely followed by Betty and little Tommy.

"You'd best get going, then," she said, opening the door on to the street.

Betty looked startled, but quickly dressed Lily and put her in the pushchair. She was silent as she helped Tommy on with his coat. The door slammed behind them as they made their way on to the pavement.

The park was only a few minutes away, and the little trio brightened up when they saw several ducks swimming about on a large pond. Lily pointed and laughed, while Tommy ran ahead excitedly until he was right at the edge of the water. They stayed there for over an hour. Betty looked at her watch. It was only ten thirty and they had another two hours before home time. Lily had fallen asleep, but Tommy was restless and bored. He'd had enough of the pond. Then it started to rain – a fine mist at first, but it soon began to get heavier with large drops falling on their bare heads.

"Oh, no, this is all we need," Betty cried, putting up the hood on the pushchair.

They began to run out of the park and along the street. There was a little café ahead, and she made for it. It was small, with just a few tables, and there were few people taking tea. Betty sat at a table near the door and helped Tommy off with his wet coat.

"You all right, love?" A large lady in a check apron was hovering over them.

"I hope you don't mind us coming in out of the rain," Betty said, searching in her purse for some coins. She wasn't sure if she had enough money for a cup of tea, but heaved a silent sigh of relief when she found a shilling and two sixpences at the bottom of the bag.

"You're new round here, aren't you? I haven't seen you before," the woman said.

"We're staying with Jesse and Tommy Price. They're my in-laws," Betty said.

"Oh, I know Tommy and Jesse. They live just two doors up from me. Tommy's a nice old chap, but Jesse can be, er, difficult. But I suppose you've found that out already," the waitress laughed.

"We only arrived last night, and we're already in her bad books," sighed Betty.

"I don't envy you, love. Never mind – this war can't go on forever. Now, what would you like – not that we have much? A bit of cake, perhaps, and I've got some home-made biscuits for the little boy."

They soon cheered up when the waitress, who was called Mabel Thorpe, brought the tea and a glass of lemonade for Tommy.

Half an hour later, the rain looked as if it might clear up. Betty peered through the café's misted-up window.

"Do you want to stay here until it's gone? It's easing off, but you'd still get soaked if you went out now," Mabel said kindly.

"Do you mind?" Betty asked anxiously. "It's just that Grandma Jesse told us not to go home until lunchtime. We've at least another hour."

"That woman!" Mabel retorted. "Never mind – come into the back for a bit. I've got a couple of comics my lad Jackie has. Perhaps Tommy might like to look at them."

They moved to a room at the back of the café, Betty feeling relief that they need not go back home before the allotted time.

A while later the rain had cleared, and Betty estimated that it would take only fifteen minutes to get home, bringing the time up to twelve thirty.

"Thank you so much, Mabel – you're a star. When I get a place of my own, you'll have to visit," Betty said, making sure that Tommy was hanging on to the pram as they left the café.

They had only gone along the pavement a few yards when a huge explosion was heard in the distance. Betty stood frozen to the spot. The bombing was here! Was she never going to get away from it? There was an eerie silence for several seconds, and then all hell broke loose. People were running from their homes into the street, and pointing at a plume of smoke that rose from the next street.

"Is that Queen Street? Is the bombing in Queen Street?" Betty looked about her wildly.

Little Tommy was crying. "Are the Jerries coming, Mum?" he shouted.

Mabel ran out of the café and herded them back inside. "You wait here, love. I'll find out what's happened," she said, rushing out of the door.

Both Tommy and Lily were crying by this time, and Betty was beginning to feel that something really bad had happened to her in-laws. Had they been at home? She thought about her husband. How would he cope if anything had happened to his parents?

Through the window she saw several people running past, then she heard the clanging of a fire-engine bell. With no more ado she gathered the children and decided to find out for herself what had happened.

Back on the street she could smell burning. The cloud of black smoke still hung in the air, and the noise was deafening as people continued to push past her.

It was then she felt a hand on her arm. Turning, she saw the blackened face of Grandma Jesse, tears streaming down her face. Thank God you're all safe," she sobbed. "I thought you might have got back home, seeing as how it was raining."

"N-no, we went in the café. Mabel kindly let us stay until the rain stopped," Betty stammered. "W-what's happened? Where is Grandpa Tommy? Was it your house that was bombed?" Betty herself was on the verge of tears.

"Tommy's all right. He wasn't at home. And yes, it was our house that got hit," Jesse said heavily. "Best come back into the café until we know more about what happened."

It wasn't until much later that they were able to get back to Queen Street. The firemen were just clearing away and the crowds had begun to disperse. Betty saw Grandpa Tommy picking through the rubble of what had once been their home. Betty couldn't believe it. Hardly anything was standing. He saw Jesse and Betty with the children and ran over to them.

"Thank God you're all safe. I got back and was told that you were all in the café," he said, putting his arms round them.

Young Tommy was looking in awe at the devastation. "Was it a big bomb, Grandpa Tommy?" he asked, bending down to retrieve something from the piles of dust.

"No, lad, it wasn't the Germans this time. We had a gas explosion, but it couldn't have done a better job if it had been a bomb," he retorted.

Just then, little Tommy silently handed something to Grandma Jesse. She gazed at it, transfixed. "Why, it's my little shepherdess. How on earth did it survive the blast?" She looked down at her grandson. "Look, love, you have it. What is a bit of china when I've got our family safe and sound!"

"And so say all of us," muttered Grandpa Tommy.

WRONG-FOOTED

If you believe in fairies, then there were both good and bad fairies at work when Lesley Jane Brown was born. The good ones bestowed on her an abundance of fair curls round a porcelain pretty face. But the bad fairies had got to work during her birth, and complications resulted in her being born with a crooked hip bone. The outcome was that Lesley was cursed with one leg being slightly shorter than the other, and no matter how skilfully made were the shoes, they failed to hide the deformity completely. On bad days, Lesley was left with a distinct limp.

"I'm sure people never notice," Lesley's mother placated. After twenty-two years she was practised at pouring balm on to her daughter's troubled spirit.

"I don't know how they can fail to notice," she wailed, holding up the offending shoe with its distinct built-up sole.

Of course, there were suitors, usually sons of local farmers. But Lesley was so lacking in confidence that she was convinced their interest lay more with her father's 10,000-acre farm than with herself.

"You're far too sensitive for your own good, my girl," her mother rebuked, after showing the door to yet another hopeful swain. No matter how she tried, she couldn't persuade her daughter that a comely face and attractive manner far outweighed any physical fault.

But Lesley was about to take things into her own hands, after seeing a dating agency advertised on the Internet. This way, she thought, they wouldn't know about the farm, and if she told them about her handicap there might be someone out there who found it didn't matter.

Later, tapping in the information about herself, she added her foot to the list of characteristics. She felt she had to be totally honest from the start. She was looking for a man with a kind, considerate nature and great sense of humour. He'd certainly need that, she thought glumly.

Thus it was, the following week found her heading for the local railway-station clock, where she was to rendezvous with a suitable date, picked out by the Hearts and Minds dating agency. She was dressed in her best hyacinth-blue suit, and sported a pink carnation in her buttonhole, as had been requested.

As she approached the clock, she could hardly believe her luck. There he was – a tall, dark and devastatingly handsome man of her dreams, sporting a pink carnation in the lapel of his immaculate dark suit.

Lesley swallowed nervously, and approached slowly so as not to exaggerate the limp.

"Hello. I'm Lesley. I believe you are waiting for me," she stuttered, feeling a hot blush rise to her cheeks.

The man turned, startled, and gazed at her uncomprehendingly for a moment.

"You're Lesley?" he asked, a stunned expression crossing his handsome features.

Lesley's face fell, her smile disappearing. "I'm sorry – I'm obviously a disappointment, not what you were expecting," she said stiffly, turning away.

"No, wait." The man grabbed her arm and grinned down at her. "It's not that you're a disappointment, just that it's a bit of a surprise – a lovely one, in fact. You're not quite the person I was led to expect. It was my own fault for assuming . . . but you're certainly an improvement on the usual sort." He tucked her arm in his, and looked at his watch. "Come on, Lesley, I think we have time for a quick drink before we get going. My car's parked just outside the station entrance."

Wordlessly, Lesley allowed him to direct her to the station bar, and after asking her what she wanted, went to the counter to order a gin and tonic for her and a lager for himself. Watching his broad back, Lesley wondered what was the usual sort he dated!

Returning to the table with the drinks, he looked at her, seemingly intrigued.

"Now tell me, Lesley, why my cousin Peter chose a girl for his best man? It's a brilliant idea, but a bit unusual to say the least. You are for real, aren't you? This isn't some kind of joke he's playing?"

Lesley sat bolt upright, rigid with shock.

"Best man? I don't understand," she croaked.

The man shook his head wonderingly. "I've been abroad and only got back yesterday. There was a phone message from my cousin asking me to pick up Leslie, his best man, who would be standing under the station clock. You're not Leslie Melwood, Peter's best man, are you?" the man said, realisation suddenly dawning." I was told Leslie would be wearing a pink carnation, but I never dreamed a girl would be there. The name Leslie can apply to both sexes, I believe."

Lesley's face had turned as pink as her carnation. Her hands flew to her mouth in horror as the truth dawned.

"My name isn't Melwood. I feel there has been a ghastly mistake. You – you're not my date from the agency, then?" she cried, feeling faint with embarrassment.

The man laughed. "Afraid not. A dating agency is hardly my scene. I'm married." He looked at her with amused sympathy. "I think we got our wires crossed. I must be picking up a male Leslie after all." He glanced swiftly at his watch. "I wondered what game Peter was playing, having a girl for his best man. Now all is clear!"

Lesley rose, knocking the table and almost spilling the drinks. Somehow her embarrassment outweighed the disappointment she felt on learning that not only was he not her date but that he had a wife!

"I must get back to the clock straight away," she said desperately. "My real date will be wondering why I haven't turned up." She was beginning to wish she had never approached the dating agency, and wondered if she could just call it a day and go home.

But the man answered for her. "We'll go back together, then, Lesley. I have to pick up the real best man – male, of course." He held out his hand. "It was lovely meeting you, Lesley, and I really wish I had been your date. He's a lucky fellow, whoever he is."

Hurrying from the bar, Lesley's limp became more pronounced at every step – a usual occurrence when she was agitated – but she didn't care any more. Her mother was right. It didn't matter that she wasn't perfect. It was the person inside that mattered, and if they were so superficial as to go by looks alone, then they were not worth knowing.

Approaching the station clock once more, she noticed two men were now standing there sporting pink carnation buttonholes. One was obviously Peter's best man, and the other one was her date, but which one was which? It was then she relaxed and smiled to herself. She knew this time which man was for her.

The computer had been accurate – too accurate, she thought wryly as she approached a pleasant curly-haired young man wearing a smart grey suit and dark shoes which almost, but didn't quite, disguise his crooked foot!

THE CAT AT BLACK TUSK

I always hankered after a brown Labrador, but it wasn't until I acquired one that I realised what I'd let myself in for. As a puppy, Ben chewed everything in sight – and I do mean everything! Rugs, carpets, wallpaper and the foot of my prized grandfather clock all came in for his undivided attention, not to mention expensive television remote-control devices, and if I left my shoes around I'd come back to find the insoles missing. He often ate what he chewed, and I wouldn't let my mind dwell on the state of his stomach!

He was an Onslow of the dog world, laid-back and lazy, and he would have been a couch potato as a human being. Having said that, however, he had certain redeeming features. Friendly beyond words, he loved other dogs, children and adults generally. As I was a bird lover and encouraged them into my garden, I turned a blind eye to his hatred of cats, and they soon learned not to stray into Ben's territory! This suited me fine, as neighbourhood cats had had the run of my garden before I moved in. Now if one so much as put a paw on the lawn, Ben would bark loudly, sending it haring for the fence. He would chase after them, but I knew he would never catch any. They were usually up and over before he even got to the flower border.

Taking Ben for a walk, however, was quite another matter. Passing houses, he would stop, sniff the air and look into the gardens to see if a cat was lurking there. I had to hold tight to his lead if he saw one sunning itself on some window sill. One house in particular always drew his attention. Set back from the lane, it had a high wrought-iron gate, with a narrow path leading up to the front door. The adjoining garage had the outline of a black elephant on the side with the words 'Black Tusk House' above it. I was intrigued. Was the owner an adventurer who had made frequent trips to Africa? I decided he must be some sort of sportsman or explorer, as in the winter his car, parked on the side drive, would hold a pair of skis on the roof rack. In summer, I noticed a couple of surfboards on the top.

But if my interest lay with the owner's pursuits, Ben's was more with the large ginger cat that often lay sunning itself on the path. Ben, straining at the leash, would bark loudly, and the cat would slink quickly through a cat flap set in the front door.

One fine summer's day, I was passing Black Tusk, tentatively searching for the ginger cat, and holding on to Ben's lead, when he suddenly squirmed out of his collar. Too late, I saw the cat on the path, just as Ben pushed his way quickly through the gate, which had been ajar. I shouted, but Ben ignored me and dashed after the cat, which had sensibly disappeared through the cat flap.

To my horror, Ben had decided not to give up on his quarry, and on reaching the door pushed his head through the cat flap! I raced up the path and tried to pull his head out of the opening, realising the difficulty of such a move as he had no collar on. After a few seconds, I succeeded in freeing him, and quickly slipped on his collar, hoping that the resident of Black Tusk wasn't about. I'd noticed with relief that the silver Honda he kept in the driveway was not there. I was just about to turn back up the path, when I heard a cry for help, which seemed to be coming from inside the house. I stopped and listened, holding on firmly to Ben's lead. I realised I hadn't been mistaken when

I heard the cry again, more loudly this time.

"Hello?" I called. "Are you all right?" – which seemed a silly thing to say to someone who was obviously in trouble.

"Thank God," the man's voice called in relief. "I thought no one would ever hear me."

"Are you hurt?" I called, my cheek against the door.

"I'm at the foot of the stairs and can't move. Do you think you could phone for an ambulance?" the man asked.

For once I was glad I had kept my mobile phone on me. Tying Ben's lead to the gatepost, I did as the man asked. Going to the door again, I tried it and found it was unlocked. I opened it, and found myself looking into a long hallway with a curved staircase. The man was lying on his side at the foot of the stairs.

"Thanks," he said gratefully. "I broke my leg a few weeks ago in a car accident, and was silly enough to slip and fall down the stairs about an hour ago. I think I've damaged the leg again. Knocked myself unconscious, too."

"It's just as well my dog doesn't like your cat," I said. "Perhaps I could help you up?"

"I think I'd better stay here until the ambulance comes. I might be a bit too heavy for you," he replied.

"It's lucky I was passing when I did, and that Ben slipped his collar. Are you on your own here?" I asked.

"My son lives with me when he comes back from university. He won't be back for another week," the man explained. "He's a big sports freak, winter and summer he's away somewhere, so I'm pretty much on my own most of the time."

"That explains the Honda I've seen sometimes parked on the driveway with all the equipment," I said. "Look, can I get you a cup of tea or something while we're waiting for the ambulance?"

"A cup of tea would be splendid! I'm Joe, by the way – Joe Halford – and my ancient cat is called Mathilda." He held out a rather weak arm, but his hand was warm and firm despite the pain he must have been in. "The kitchen's on the right."

"I'm Kirsty Stoneman, and my naughty dog is called Ben," I replied.

"Well, you can thank Ben from me for finding me like this. I might have been here for some time," Joe said warmly.

I repaired to the kitchen. It was surprisingly neat and tidy for a man living on his own, and I soon found cups, tea, milk and sugar, and put the kettle on to boil.

"I only live in the next lane, and pass here quite a bit. I'm always intrigued by the name of your house," I said a few minutes later, handing him a mug of tea.

He sipped it slowly, his hand trembling slightly.

"Black Tusk? Oh, there's nothing particularly exotic about it. I named the house after a wildlife park my late wife and I visited when we were in Canada a few years ago."

"A wildlife park!" I laughed. "And I thought it was named after an African adventure."

"No such luck," Joe answered wryly. "I leave the adventure to my son. I'm a humble accountant, semi-retired."

Just then there was the sound of the ambulance pulling up on the driveway.

"Sounds like it's here," Joe said, setting his mug down on the stairs.

"Look, Kirsty, I know it might be an imposition, but do you think you could come in and feed Mathilda while I'm in hospital?" Joe was looking at me apprehensively.

"Of course I'll see to Mathilda – minus Ben, of course." I smiled. "Don't worry, Joe – it's no trouble at all. I'm semi-retired, too."

After Joe and the ambulance departed, I unhooked an impatient Ben from the gatepost and made my way home, after making sure the cat had been fed and watered, and locking the front door.

I later phoned the hospital, but couldn't get any information as I wasn't a relative, so the next day decided to visit Joe just to reassure him that Mathilda was being cared for.

I found they had placed Joe in a room on his own. His leg up in a sling, he was looking worse than he had done at the foot of the stairs. He opened his eyes as I approached the bed, and grinned weakly.

"Fractured my skull and didn't know it," he croaked. "I think I might be in here for longer than I anticipated." He looked at me, a troubled expression on his face. "Look, Kirsty, my son Peter won't be back for a few days. He knows about the accident, but I reassured him I was OK. In the meantime, could you continue to feed Mathilda for me?"

I patted his arm. "Don't worry, Joe – Mathilda will be looked after until your son returns. You shouldn't worry. Try to relax and get better."

He smiled and lay back on the pillow, closing his eyes. "I'm so glad we met. But I wish it had been in better circumstances," he murmured, and he appeared to be dropping off to sleep.

"I'm glad we met, too, Joe," I replied quietly, heading for the door. I meant it, too. There was something about Joe that I warmed to instantly.

A few days later I was able to hand over the feeding of Mathilda to Joe's son, a tall muscular youth with a shock of blonde hair and an infectious grin like his father's.

"Thanks for taking care of Dad's cat, Kirsty. He doesn't have many neighbours round here, as most of them are students renting out rooms in some of the houses. I hate to think what could have happened if you hadn't found him. He was quite badly hurt, you know, but I think he's on the mend now."

"Yes, he seems quite tough. Anyway, Mathilda's all yours. Every time I return home after feeding her, Ben gives me suspicious looks. He knows I've been with her," I laughed.

"I'm not sure where she came from – just turned up on Dad's

doorstep a few years ago. The vet seems to think she is quite old, maybe sixteen," Peter explained.

"She can certainly move for an old cat. The only time Ben moves fast is when he's chasing a cat, and he's never got even close to Mathilda," I said.

A month later, my front doorbell rang, and on opening it I found Joe standing there, a big bunch of pink roses in his arms. I noticed he was walking with a stick.

"Oh, it's good to see you're out of hospital, Joe!" I exclaimed. "Do come in."

Sitting at the kitchen table, he thrust the flowers into my hands. "I do feel this is no way nearly enough for what I owe you. Helping me after the fall, and then feeding my cat!"

"Look, it was no trouble at all. Like you I'm semi-retired. I work in a solicitor's office three mornings a week. I started there three years ago after my husband, Ted, died. It keeps me busy. . . ." My voice trailed off. I felt I'd been talking too much and Joe certainly wouldn't be concerned with my life.

But he did seem interested. "Have you any children, grandchildren?" he asked.

I shook my head slowly.

"Ted and I would have loved to have had a family, but a serious illness he had when he was young made it impossible for him to father a child. But he ended up as headmaster of a junior school, so had plenty of children to keep him occupied," I chuckled.

"And you? What did you do to occupy your life?" Joe asked softly.

"Well," I said, feeling slightly embarrassed," I was a legal secretary for several years. It was interesting – but a bit dull. Anyway, that's enough about me. How is Mathilda? I haven't seen her around when I've passed the house."

Joe looked sad. "She disappeared a few days ago. Peter and I have searched the entire neighbourhood, and beyond – no luck!

She hadn't been well, and I'd taken her to the vet's a couple of times. He didn't think she would last long. She was a very old cat. We think she may have gone somewhere to die quietly on her own. Animals are known to do that sometimes."

"What a pity, Joe. I'd become quite attached to her, even if Ben didn't agree! She was a lovely-natured cat. Will you get another one eventually?"

Joe looked at me, and then at Ben, who had retired to his basket when he realised there were no treats on offer. "I don't think so," he said slowly. Then, with a mischievous grin on his face, he added, "Ben doesn't like cats, so if I'm to get to know you better, another cat at Black Tusk may be one too many!"

DAUGHTERS

Looking back, I now realise that I really lost my daughter when she was three years old. She'd been delighted with a rocking horse she received on her second birthday, so I thought a ride on a real pony would be a treat for her third. The moment she was placed on the pony, with her feet barely reaching the stirrups, she was transformed! From then on, horses were her life to the exclusion of everything else. Some girls grow out of horses when they reach their teenage years and boys start to come into the picture, but not Lyndsay!

"Your cousin Shirley is having a disco for her eighteenth and you've been invited," I said cautiously, knowing what the answer might be.

"I'd love to, Mum, but we've got the show coming up and I've a lot to do at the stables," she replied, rushing out of the room, riding hat in hand.

Her own eighteenth birthday was next, but she was far too busy to have a party, and I ended up watching her compete in a showjumping class at the county arena. She came a commendable second, considering she was up against a group of highly ambitious riders who seemed to get a huge amount of support from their parents. The parents, I noted, were highly knowledgeable about equine matters and had provided all the necessary equipment, from luxurious horseboxes, complete with living accommodation, to expensive saddles. They seemed to have everything needed to make them winners. Seeing Lyndsay with her small borrowed horsebox and the beat-up old four-by-four she used to transport it, I felt guilty. I had never had the money to help her in this way. She had had to get a job in the local riding and livery stables to afford Star, the chestnut which was her pride and joy.

But to tell the truth, I was nervous around horses. I always seemed to be sidestepping some highly strung filly which seemed hell-bent on crushing my foot beneath a prancing hoof. I was also worried about my daughter. Supposing she fell off and was badly injured, or a horse kicked her on the head when she was tending a hoof? Accidents happened all the time, didn't they? I just felt sad that I was unable to help her in her chosen career, but I knew there was no turning back. She loved what she was doing, and it was too late to try and persuade her to take up something else.

By the time she was twenty-eight I had resigned myself to her never getting married and having children. She was a tall, beautiful young woman with a mane of red hair, but there didn't seem to be any man on the horizon.

From assisting at the local stables, Lyndsay had by this time acquired her own little riding school, teaching local children to ride on their own mounts. It was therefore quite a surprise when one fine spring morning she turned up with a man in tow. His name was James, the son of a local farmer, and within a year they had moved in together, renting a converted barn on the edge of the village. However, although they were obviously in love and happily settled, there was never any mention of marriage. As for children, I was told in no uncertain terms that a family was not on the cards. Sadly, I had to come to terms with the fact that I would never see my daughter walk down the aisle as a bride, and I would never be a grandmother either.

I envied my two sisters, Carol and Jill. They each had a daughter, and the girls had never shown any interest in anything but boys and wanting to start a family. Carol's daughter, Shirley, had two children, a boy and a girl, and Anne, Jill's daughter, had two little sons.

"It's a shame Lyndsay has never wanted children, Janet," Carol said on one of her frequent visits. "My grandchildren mean everything to me. It's funny not wanting to be a mother. I thought all girls wanted children." She glanced at me pityingly.

"Not all girls, Carol. Lyndsay is happy as she is, and I can't see her changing her mind now," I replied defensively.

She took a sip of her tea before placing the cup carefully on the saucer. "Mind you, I sometimes think you're better off with things as they are." She smiled ruefully.

"You can't mean that after having two lovely grandchildren! They're a credit to Shirley and her husband, and you'd be lost without them," I protested. At the same time I had wondered why Carol had looked upset when she arrived.

"You don't know the half of it, Janet. Things aren't as rosy as you think they are."

"What's happened, Carol? I thought Shirley had forgiven Bob for his, er, misdemeanours," I said, concerned by the look on her face.

"Is that what you call it?" she answered curtly. "I call it being unfaithful to my daughter when she was eight months pregnant!"

"I thought that had all blown over, and things were back to normal after Ruby's birth," I said.

Carol shook her head. "He's at it again. Shirley tells me he didn't come home on Saturday night. Turned up midday on Sunday without any explanation, and walked out on her yesterday. Took all his clothes. She's heartbroken."

"Oh, Carol, I'm so sorry. What's going to happen to Shirley and the children now?" I asked, suddenly feeling sick with worry for my sister and her family.

Carol sighed. "The house is mortgaged to the hilt, and

apparently he's not paid anything for the past three months. Shirley wants to move back in with me and Bill."

Remembering Carol's small three-bedroomed semi, I couldn't help feeling sorry for her.

"How are you going to cope?"

"It seems we'll have to. Bill isn't happy. He likes a bit of peace and quiet since he took early retirement, and It won't be easy having a couple of young grandchildren running about the place. It will be all right with Robbie being at school, but Ruby's only two and she's a handful at the moment – into everything." Carol was looking decidedly miserable.

"Perhaps Shirley will get a job. Didn't she take a secretarial course when she left school?" I asked.

"Oh, yes, and everything was fine until she met that Lothario and got married at seventeen. You know, Janet, she's never worked. She'll have to start from scratch, but how she'll manage that with two young children, and employment being what it is at the moment, I don't know." She sighed and took another sip of her tea.

Later, watching her walk down the path, shoulders hunched, I really pitied her. Both Shirley and Anne lived close to their parents. It was a set-up I had always envied, as my sisters always saw a great deal of their grandchildren, but I wasn't sure I'd want Carol's problem right now.

A week later I saw the familiar figure of my younger sister, Jill, trudging up the path. Like Carol, she had had her fair share of trouble with her daughter Anne, and, from the thunderous look on her face, it would seem her problems were far from over. Seated in the front room with a cup of tea in front of her, Jill began to cry.

Concerned, I put my arm round her. "What on earth's the matter, Jill? It's unlike you to break down?"

Taking a large tissue from her pocket she blew her nose

noisily and wiped her eyes. "It's Anne," she sniffed.

Somehow that didn't surprise me. Jill's daughter had been trouble from the age of fourteen, shoplifting and drug taking before becoming pregnant at sixteen. Now twenty-one, she was still a worry for her mother.

"What has she done this time?" I asked, dreading the answer.

"It's not what she's done, it's what he's done!" Jill wailed, referring to Anne's live-in boyfriend, an alcoholic, who was not the father of her two sons. "He's given her a black eye and two broken ribs, and refuses to budge from the flat."

I sighed. "You always said he was no good, Jill. Didn't he hit her once before?"

"Yes," sobbed my sister. "I warned her about him, but you know what she's like. She's always done her own thing. This wouldn't have happened if Tony had been alive."

Tony, Jill's husband, had died when Anne was only ten, and Jill had never married again, more's the pity. Young Anne had missed her father, who could have helped guide her through those difficult teenage years. She was too high-spirited for her mother to deal with. Jill was too soft-hearted, and Anne had always traded on it.

"The council flat is in Anne's name, isn't it? She should notify the council and have him evicted. It must be horrible for the children to see their mother abused in this way," I said angrily.

Jill dried her eyes again and sipped her tea. "That's what I've told her to do, and I think she's listening this time."

"Good," I said.

Just then the phone rang. It was like a breath of fresh air to hear my daughter's voice on the other end.

"Hi, Mum. James and I haven't seen you for a while. We're thinking of popping over tomorrow. Is that all right?" she chirped happily.

"Of course, darling. You know you are both welcome any time," I replied.

"Good. We'll be over just as soon as I've seen to the horses."

She rang off before I could say anything else. Lyndsay was not the kind of daughter to have long chats with her mother over the phone, I thought ruefully, remembering the times I had been at my sisters' homes and had to wait half an hour or more while they chatted animatedly to their daughters, despite the girls living just a few streets away.

Even so, where daughters were concerned, I had no right to feel disappointed with mine. Yes, I would have liked to have had a conventional daughter who wanted to marry and have children, but hey, having daughters didn't give us the right to set an agenda for them to follow. With luck, they could end up happily married with healthy, intelligent children for grandmothers to dote on. But we didn't live in an ideal world. We had to accept things as they were, even when, despite our efforts in trying to bring them up to our standards, life didn't turn out as we had hoped. We could only support them for so long, and be there to pick up the pieces if lives were shattered.

In many ways, I felt lucky to have a daughter like Lyndsay, who was happy with her life. I was never going to be a grandmother, but I could help my sisters with their grandchildren. That was what families were about.

I turned to Jill, sitting miserably on my sofa as Carol had done the week before. I put a comforting arm round her shoulders. "Things will turn out fine in the end, Jill, just you see," I said. "Daughters, eh? Who'd have 'em!"

THE TOWNIE

From the bedroom window, Carol could see the gulls swooping and soaring, like bits of torn white paper caught in the strong March wind. Ted was somewhere under those birds, faithfully ploughing the six-acre field. 'But we won't be here to see the crops grow,' she thought bitterly.

She sat down on the bed. It was early and yet she was already feeling tired.

"I'm no use to him like this," she muttered aloud. "He needs someone strong and capable – someone to help out and stand by his side as he farms this land. Now more than ever."

"I hope you know what you're letting yourself in for, lass." Ted's father's voice came back to haunt her. "The womenfolk round here are all from farming stock. They know what it's all about. It can be a hard life and a lonely one, especially for a townie like yourself."

A townie! Yes, and he might have added a puny one at that, with her fair, wispy hair and fragile frame. But despite the warning, she and Ted had gone ahead and were wildly happy on their wedding day five years ago. In the beginning things were fine. She turned out to be surprisingly strong, in spite of the apparently delicate bone structure, and even Ted's father had been impressed with the way she had tackled everything.

They teased her because she fed the crows – black sentinels

that seemed to stand guard over the oak trees that surrounded the farm.

"But they need food, just like any other creature," she protested when her father-in-law chided her. "Besides, if they weren't so hungry they wouldn't peck out the eyes of the young lambs come the spring," she added hopefully.

Ted shook his head and laughed, but he took the shotgun with him just the same. They had to keep the numbers down, particularly foxes, rabbits and magpies. The list seemed endless, and she never got used to the easy way in which country folk disposed of those creatures which threatened their livelihood.

Ted's father died three years into their marriage, and suddenly Ted was on his own with a wife who wasn't much use, and when the subsidies were cut they had to reduce the hours of their one farmhand.

"I can barely manage to pay our way as it is," Ted had reasoned, a worried frown creasing his suntanned brow.

So they had struggled on, until she became pregnant.

"Don't worry, love – I'll get Frank in part-time. We'll manage," Ted had tried to reassure her, but she knew her pregnancy had come at a very bad time.

But the baby never stirred within her, and at six months she went into labour, knowing that the baby was dead. It had seemed like a bad omen then. The following year the crops were poor because of the heavy rains, and an outbreak of TB decimated Ted's herd of prize Friesians.

"It will take years to build up the herd again." Ted's voice sounded hollow, defeated.

Now they were struggling for their very existence, and Ted had decided to give up the farm that had been in his family for generations.

"The longer we stay, the deeper in debt I'll be," Ted informed her, a note of desperation in his voice.

His morale was dealt a further blow when they learned of the suicide of an old farming friend of Ted's father.

"I can't imagine old Jim doing a thing like that. He was always such a strong character." Ted's voice cracked with emotion.

This tragic news seemed to depress him more than anything else, and he became silent, withdrawn, unable to communicate with her any more. Even the unexpected news that she was pregnant again – something they had both wanted with mixed emotions – failed to raise his spirits. In fact, the news seemed to make him more withdrawn. He became a wooden figure about the farm, going through the motions, but the spirit seemed to have been drained from him. She felt that the baby, rather than being a joy, was to Ted simply another financial burden. If only he would talk!

She could hear the distant rumble of the tractor, and wearily sank back on to the pillows. She felt guilty at her lethargy, but knew better than to struggle against it. The doctor had assured her that tiredness early on was normal. But it was almost six months and she still felt drained.

"You'll definitely have to take it easy this time, Mrs Bower. We don't want a repetition of last time, do we?" Dr Bellamy had patted her hand comfortingly during her antenatal visit the previous day. "When you feel tired, you should rest. Don't overdo it. There's no reason why you shouldn't have a healthy baby at the end of it."

The doctor's parting words echoed in her mind. They hadn't brought any comfort. She couldn't take it easy! Their financial troubles and her fears about having another stillborn baby were like a two-pronged fork, prodding at and destroying any vestige of happiness. Eventually, exhausted, she fell into a deep sleep.

She awoke to a strangely silent world. The light was

beginning to go, and looking at the bedside clock she realised it was almost six. She couldn't hear the tractor, or the gulls. She lay there, her ears straining for the familiar farm sounds, but there was only silence. She struggled from the bed and moved clumsily to the window. The tractor was standing in the middle of the field, apparently abandoned. Where was Ted? Fear raked her heart. He would never leave a piece of precious farm machinery in the field without good reason.

Carefully she descended the steep wooden staircase and entered the kitchen. The kettle was cold, and there was no sign that he had been there. She struggled into her waterproof coat and moved into the yard. The sky was losing that strange, bright opalescence of early spring, and a chill breeze ruffled the heads of the daffodils she had planted along the hedge a couple of years ago. Only that wind in the boughs of the oaks, and the sharp cawing of a crow, broke the silence.

The clay soil stuck to her boots as she struggled across the neatly ploughed furrows to the stranded tractor. The bonnet was cold to the touch. She turned away, suddenly feeling terribly afraid. Ted had been really depressed lately, but had refused to see a doctor. What if? Her mind was trying to reject what her heart was telling her, yet she started to run. The river was only a couple of hundred yards away over the brow of the hill. It acted as a boundary between their farm and the Lassiters' spread.

The going was hard and she was almost out of breath when she reached the bank. The river was swollen by recent rains, but as she looked down her heart froze. Ted's shirt! Even from a distance, soaked in river water and streaked with mud, she could make out the distinctive red check pattern. It was his favourite, and although well worn he had refused to part with it. Sobbing now, her hair whipped in damp strands about her pale face, she flopped down on the muddy ground, her eyes scanning the rapidly flowing water. There was no sign of him.

Crying wildly now, she slowly rose and half dragged herself back to the farm. She had to get help. Ted might still be alive! But even as hope flickered it was extinguished by the reality of the situation. The current was strong, and the river was known to be treacherous even at its lowest point. If Ted was in there, then they would only recover his body.

She somehow reached the door of the farmhouse kitchen, stopping to draw breath. It was then she heard it – the singing of the kettle! She burst into the room and almost collapsed with relief at the sight of Ted spooning tea into the teapot. He turned and gazed at her in shock.

"Where on earth have you been? Look at you, you're soaked and covered in mud, and there was I thinking you were still in bed. I was about to bring you up a cup of tea!" he exclaimed, folding her in his arms.

"Oh, Ted!" She burst out sobbing again, this time the relief turning her shaking limbs to jelly. "I thought you were drowned in the river. The tractor was abandoned and—" Further words were buried in his jacket as he held her close.

"Silly crow woman!" He laughed softly, trying to dry her tears. "You were fast asleep when I came in to tell you I was going with Lassiter to see the bank manager. I didn't want to disturb you. Anyway, I think things might be looking up. With Lassiter's support the bank has agreed to a loan for a riding centre. Lassiter wants me to go into partnership with him. We're diversifying, and at least it will help to keep us going until things get better."

She broke away to look at his dear face, which was looking more cheerful and optimistic than she had seen for a long time.

Suddenly, his face became serious again. "What on earth made you think I had drowned? You don't think I could have left you and the baby, do you?"

She looked down, suddenly feeling guilty that she could

have doubted him. "It was your check shirt. It was in the river."

Ted looked startled, and then started to laugh.

"Don't you remember? You kept nagging me about it, so I put it on the old scarecrow in the barley field last month. It must have blown into the river during the gales."

For a moment she closed her eyes, a relieved smile lighting up her face. Suddenly, her eyes flew open in shock. "Ted, Ted, I felt the baby. The baby actually gave a little push then. I felt it!"

"After what you've just put him through, I'm not surprised," Ted replied, grinning as he placed a gentle hand on her abdomen. "Things are going to be better for all of us from now on," he promised.

AURAS

Jessie was very good at auras. They were there, all around her, glowing halos over people's heads. Not with animals, you understand. No, animals don't have proper auras. They all have the same greyish glow, which is completely different to the human aura.

Jessie's gift – for a gift it was – arrived when she was barely into her teens. The first aura appeared round her mother. A soft, glowing pink it was, a delicate feminine shade which matched her mother's delicate characteristics. A soft woman, a woman's woman, who had been unable to match the passionate needs of her gregarious husband, Rolf. Jessie hadn't seen much of her father while she was growing up. He had gone off with the earthy Janna. Later, when she was seventeen, she had met up with her father again, soon after the death of her mother. She had been spellbound by the strong crimsons, oranges and purples of his aura, matched only by the fiery glow emanating from the sexy Janna. Yes, they were a perfect couple, conceded Jessie. Her mother's delicacy had been no match for that!

When she left school, Jessie found it difficult to make friends, mainly because of her gift. She knew immediately the type of character a person was, simply by looking at the colour of their aura. Several girls in the typing pool she later joined were often bathed in varying shades of green. There was a lot of jealousy and backbiting amongst them, particularly over the handsome head of department, Rupert Gumbold. But on seeing Rupert's bright red aura, Jessie took an instant dislike to him. Behind that charming facade lurked a violent temper.

Then there was the local vicar, who surprised her by having an aura of crimson and mauve when she had expected a more pastel hue. So, a passionate nature lurked behind that virtuous, sanctimonious facade, she thought.

Jessie particularly liked Hazel's, a colleague's aura of golden yellow, suitable for a girl with so sunny a nature, who never had a bad word to say against anyone. They had become good friends.

When it came to choosing a partner, though, Jessie knew she would have a problem, particularly if she initially liked a person and then found that his aura didn't match up. But in many ways it would eventually make choosing a life partner easier. There was no pulling the wool over her eyes!

She turned down the charming Ian, with his gentle good looks. The dark grey aura surrounding him bode ill for their future. The generous Sam seemed a fitting choice, but his smiling countenance didn't deceive her! His aura had been almost black, denoting a manic depressive lurking there. Then there had been Joe, a wise-cracking young man with an easy manner. Unfortunately, his blue aura told her that his apparent warmth masked a cold nature.

But just as she was despairing of ever finding a soulmate, she met Robert. She knew at once he was the right man for her. A halo of gentle rainbow colours lit his countenance – a rainbow which, when she looked in the mirror, exactly matched the one above her own head!